ALSO BY MARCY DERMANSKY

Hurricane Girl
Very Nice
The Red Car
Bad Marie
Twins

Hot
Air

HOT
AIR

Marcy Dermansky

ALFRED A. KNOPF * NEW YORK

A BORZOI BOOK
FIRST HARDCOVER EDITION
PUBLISHED BY ALFRED A. KNOPF 2025

Published by Alfred A. Knopf, a division of Penguin Random House LLC,
1745 Broadway, New York, NY 10019.

Knopf, Borzoi Books, and the colophon are registered trademarks
of Penguin Random House LLC.

LIBRARY OF CONGRESS CATALOGING-IN-PUBLICATION DATA
Names: Dermansky, Marcy, [dates] author.
Title: Hot air : a novel / Marcy Dermansky.
Description: First United States edition. | New York :
Alfred A. Knopf, 2025.
Identifiers: LCCN 2024006462 (print) | LCCN 2024006463 (ebook) |
ISBN 9780593320907 (hardcover) | ISBN 9780593315361 (paperback) |
ISBN 9780593320914 (ebook)
Subjects: LCGFT: Romance fiction. | Bawdy fiction. | Novels.
Classification: LCC PS3604.E7545 H68 2025 (print) |
LCC PS3604.E7545 (ebook) | DDC 813/.6—dc23/eng/20240223
LC record available at https://lccn.loc.gov/2024006462
LC ebook record available at https://lccn.loc.gov/2024006463

penguinrandomhouse.com | aaknopf.com

Printed in the United States of America
10 9 8 7 6 5 4 3 2 1

The authorized representative in the EU for product safety and
compliance is Penguin Random House Ireland, Morrison Chambers,
32 Nassau Street, Dublin D02 YH68, Ireland,
https://eu-contact.penguin.ie.

For Nina

Hot
Air

Joannie was not certain how the date was going. She had not been on a date for a very long time. Not since her divorce seven years ago. And then, of course, not during her ten years of marriage. She had never been on a proper date with her ex-husband even before they were married. He had just sort of worn her down, so clearly in love with her.

And that was a big chunk of her life.

Her marriage.

Years and years of her life. Stolen. Not only the opportunity to date, but to lead her life, spend her days the way she would have liked, instead of always trying to placate someone else. She did, of course, have a marvelous child. Lucy.

So, she was on a date. Joannie had met him not on an app but in real life, at a block party on a very fancy block around the corner from her not-that-fancy apartment. Her daughter had a friend who lived on this block. At the party, Joannie had gotten pleasantly drunk and accepted a hit from a joint, even though she did not like to smoke pot, because she figured, why not? Some people made friends through their dogs. Joannie met people through her daughter. The man she'd met had a son the same age as her daughter, and her daughter said this boy wasn't awful.

Johnny texted her the next day, asking her out, and when Joannie replied that she did not have a babysitter, he wrote back that she should come to his house, bring her daughter, and the kids could watch a movie in the basement. He promised a nice meal, and Joannie loved free dinners. Nothing, of course, could ever happen between them because of their names. Joannie and Johnny.

Joannie realized very quickly that she was not attracted to Johnny. He was not unattractive. Attractive, even. He had money, too, which was important after being married for so long to a man who did not. He liked good movies. He read books. He had made her dinner. She knew, however, that she was not attracted to him, because after the meal, he had kissed her. They had gone outside to watch the sunset. The sky had turned pink. The light sparkled over the lawn, onto the swimming pool that Joannie did not know he had. She returned the kiss. It started out fine and then became unpleasant—oppressive, even—with Johnny's tongue in her mouth, his arms wrapped around her so tightly that it was difficult to extricate herself. It was a kiss that did not end. Joannie was realizing that she would have to forcibly end this kiss, because she would soon require oxygen, when a hot air balloon came veering down toward Johnny's very large backyard. "Holy fuck!" Johnny yelled, letting her go, looking up at the sky, while Joannie gulped for air.

The hot air balloon was heading straight for the swimming pool. It was crazy. Joannie decided she was never going to kiss this man, Johnny, again.

This made her sad, because during the meal, she had begun to imagine their life together, and already it had come crashing down. Like a hot air balloon. She had thought about the flowers she would plant in the yard, the coffee she would drink in the morning, sitting outside in one of the Adirondack chairs beneath the oak tree. The basement had a fully equipped playroom with a floor-to-ceiling movie screen. She would be a stepmother, which was tricky, but how hard could that be? It would be nice to have a playmate for her daughter. But now she would never find out.

There was a man and a woman in the basket of the hot air balloon careering from the sky, and they were screaming, not out of fear, but in anger. They seemed to hate each other. They were all dressed up.

"Make way!"

"We're coming down!"

"I will kill you, if we don't die!"

This was startling, to say the least.

"They are going to land in the pool!" Johnny said. He and Joannie ran for the pool, but the hot air balloon landed on the lawn, right at the edge of the pool.

"Thank God!" Johnny yelled.

"We're okay!" the man yelled.

And then the balloon tipped over, falling into the pool with a poignant splash. The man went under, headfirst. Joannie watched the bottoms of his leather shoes go under last. She had never seen anything like this.

Joannie was grateful not to be kissing Johnny anymore, and a man had fallen into the pool and needed saving. Joannie dove in. It was mid-May. The water was cold. She grabbed the man, putting her arms around his chest, and brought him up to the surface, kicking with her legs, and there at the end of the pool was Johnny and the woman in an evening gown, who had somehow climbed out of the basket onto dry land, and they were helping her pull the man out of the water. He began spouting water. Not dead. Not in need of CPR, which was a relief, because Joannie did not know how to give CPR. He was wearing a tuxedo.

Joannie pulled herself out of the pool on her own, while Johnny and the woman from the hot air balloon tended to the not-drowned man. Joannie could not believe how alive she felt. She felt amazing. She had saved a man's life. She had jumped into cold water. It was a tremendous combination. She could feel the grin on her face. She saw Johnny looking up at her and her smile extended to him. Maybe she would try kissing him again. Maybe she had been wrong.

"That was incredible," she said.

Joannie wondered about her daughter, wondered if she had

seen the hot air balloon go into the pool, but the kids were in the windowless basement, watching the third Harry Potter movie.

—

The man in the tuxedo looked familiar to Joannie. She did not think that she knew him. Possibly he was famous.

"Joannie?" he said.

Joannie blinked.

She *did* know him.

From the news, yes, but also from sleepaway camp, a long time ago. He had been a dick. She had hated him.

"It's Jonathan," he said. "Jonathan Foster. It's been a long time. We went to camp together."

Joannie's first kiss had been with this man, when she was fourteen, when he was not the CEO of a major tech company. The kiss had taken place on the first day of camp. They were waiting for an activity to start and somehow instead took a walk around the camp, and they were behind the dining hall when he asked if he could kiss her. He was so good-looking, and he liked her, and it had been a good kiss, even—Joannie had felt her skin tingle—but that had been it. They never kissed again; they did not even hang out. They barely talked to each other. Jonathan had his group, the popular kids, and Joannie had hers, the oddballs and losers. Camp had been a lot like school that way. He never acknowledged that they'd ever kissed. It left Joannie doubting herself, wondering if it had ever happened. Had he kissed her? Had she imagined it? She was surprised that he remembered her name.

"You just saved my life," he said. "Oh my God. Joannie

Nelson. Can you believe sometimes I still think about you?"

He said it like it was a gift, like this would mean something to her, which seemed crazy. His ego was astounding.

"That's weird," Joannie said. "I don't ever think about you."

The moment that followed felt awkward.

How were you supposed to behave after a hot air balloon crashed into a swimming pool on your first date in many years? This was new territory for Joannie. As a rule, Joannie didn't like rich people, but she thought that could change if she were to become one.

"My name is Jonathan, too," Johnny said. "But people call me Johnny. Welcome. Way to make an entrance, man."

The woman in the evening gown took off her high heels. She did not join the conversation. Instead, she walked over to the table where Johnny and Joannie had taken their drinks outside, picked up the bottle of red wine, and took a long slug. The group collectively stared at the hot air balloon that had sunk to the bottom of the pool.

"I have always hated anniversaries," the woman said. "But this one was too much. Seriously, Jonathan, I'm done."

Jonathan sighed.

"I was trying to make a grand romantic gesture," he said.

"And you failed," his wife said. "Miserably."

"You told me you liked this idea."

"So it's my fault."

The wife had straight shoulder-length brown hair. She had bangs. She had blue eyes. She looked, honestly, a little bit like Joannie.

Jonathan, for that matter, resembled Johnny. They were middle-aged white men in decent shape. Maybe they were all interchangeable. Maybe, Joannie thought, this date was getting interesting.

"Would you have anything dry that I could change into?" Jonathan asked.

"Seriously," the woman said. "That's what you care about?"

"I am wet," Jonathan said. "What's wrong with that?"

"Where are my manners?" Johnny said. "Of course I do. Give me a second. I'll gather some clothes."

"I think I had better go home," Joannie said. "I need dry clothes, too."

"No! Don't go!" Johnny cried. They had been kissing, Joannie remembered. She had not liked the kiss, but maybe he had. He did not seem particularly perceptive. "I'll find something for you, too, Joannie. This night is just getting started. This is a night like no other! I have a hot air balloon at the bottom of my swimming pool! And unexpected guests! I'm going to find some dry clothes for everyone. We can check to see if the kids are okay, and then keep the party going."

"I don't think this can be considered a party," Joannie said, regretting how unkind she sounded.

It was possible that Johnny was an idiot.

It was possible that Jonathan and his wife had suffered some sort of trauma. But they seemed fine. Johnny and Jonathan went into the house together in search of dry clothing.

Joannie knew that she should go check on Lucy. But once she did that, she would be a mom again, and it felt good to have a few hours off. Johnny had a point, really. About continuing the night. Anyway, where were the sirens? Concerned neighbors?

Johnny did have very large hedges.

⟋

The wife sat down at the end of the pool. She dangled her feet in the water. She continued to drink wine from the bottle. It must have been frightening, falling from the sky. Joannie had never been in a hot air balloon. "This night was a disaster from beginning to end," the wife said to Joannie. "But this wine is very good. So there is that."

"And it's your anniversary," Joannie said. "That adds a lot of pressure."

"Have you fucked my husband?" the wife asked.

Joannie shook her head, surprised by the wife's bluntness. "No. Of course not. We kissed once when we were fourteen."

"Oh," the wife said. "Don't get me wrong. I don't actually want to fuck my husband. I just get peeved that he fucks around. The world goes a little bit back to normal, and boom, he starts fucking again."

"That makes sense to me," Joannie said, and it did. "How long have you been married?"

"Five years."

So, not as long as Joannie had been married. Five years was nothing compared to ten. Marriage was an institution that sucked you in whole, would not easily let you out.

"And it's your anniversary," Joannie said again.

Joannie had also hated anniversaries. There was so much pressure to be in love. Her ex-husband always wanted to do something. Cook a special dinner. Go out for a special dinner. No matter what—no matter what you ate or where you ate it— the night was supposed to end with sex. Maybe all marriages should end naturally the moment you realize that you have no interest in ever having sex with your spouse again. Unless, she supposed, the feeling was mutual.

"Maybe," Joannie said, "the night will get better."

She did not believe this, but she wanted to fill the uncomfortable silence.

"It's possible," the wife said.

Joannie took off her wet jeans and sat down next to the wife, putting her feet in the pool as well. She wondered if Johnny understood how lucky he was. To have his own swimming pool.

"I'm Joannie," Joannie said.

"Julia." The wife, who was no longer the wife but Julia, started to laugh. "Johnny, Joannie, Jonathan, and Julia. The four J's," she said.

Joannie laughed, too.

She felt strangely happy.

She accepted the wine bottle from Julia. It *was* good wine, expensive wine, and she drank. Soon they would have to open another bottle.

The hot air balloon at the bottom of the pool was a problem to solve, but it was not her problem. Johnny was taking a long time with the dry clothes. She took off her shirt and slid back into the pool. It was better than sitting in her wet clothes.

"You're crazy," Julia said appreciatively.

"I love to swim," Joannie said.

She really did. This was her first swim of the season. She sank under the water—it really was cold—pushed her legs against the back of the pool, and swam the length of it without taking a breath, circling the hot air balloon. Though she had not been planning to, she swam some laps. Back and forth and back and forth again. She had made it through this long, scary year, lockdowns and quarantine, all alone in an apartment with her child, filled with fear and envying her rich neighbors and their big houses. She had not even known that so many of them had swimming pools in their backyards. It was probably better not to have known. She would have been seething.

Joannie swam and swam.

When she stopped, she noticed all of them looking at her, Johnny and Jonathan and Julia.

"That felt good," Joannie said.

"Glad to hear it," Johnny said, always amiable. He was incredibly amiable. He had a large towel ready for Joannie, which she gratefully accepted. Jonathan had already changed into dry clothes. A gray sweatshirt and blue sweatpants. Johnnie had the same outfit for her. He seemed to have a Lands' End sweatshirt collection.

"The kids are good," he told her. "They want to have a sleepover."

"Really?" Joannie asked. Lucy had never played with this boy, Tyson, before. It had been a long time since her last sleepover.

"What about you two?" Johnny extended his arms to Jonathan and Julia. "I have a guest room. We can deal with this mess in the morning," Johnny said, gesturing toward the hot air balloon at the bottom of the pool.

The sun had set. Joannie realized that it had gotten dark outside.

"Fine with me," Julia said.

Joannie was surprised. Maybe this woman did not want to be alone with her husband. Jonathan, she noticed, annoyed with herself for noticing, was handsome. She had been comparing so many kisses unfavorably to her first kiss. She was sure that he would want to leave. They had to live somewhere fabulous.

"Fine with you," Jonathan said.

"I do not want to step into another moving vehicle with you tonight," she said.

"Ouch," Johnny said.

Joannie wondered how Jonathan would respond.

"Okay," Jonathan said. "I guess I'm in. Sleepover."

Joannie wanted to go home—the idea of sleeping alone in an empty apartment, leaving Lucy in the basement with her new friend for the night, was appealing—but then Julia insisted Joannie stay, too.

"Don't leave," she said. "We need you."

"Yes," Johnny agreed. "Don't leave."

Jonathan shrugged.

They needed her.

And Joannie found Julia appealing. The chances were good that back at her apartment, she would end up cleaning, because she had left it a mess. As always. And this night had taken an interesting turn. She could not remember the last time that had happened. The last time anything interesting had happened. She agreed to stay.

Joannie wondered where she would sleep. Was there

another guest room for her? How big was this house? Johnny leaned back in his chair. He beamed at her. He must have thought it was a good kiss.

"It's wild about you and Jonathan," Julia said. "I love coincidences like this."

"This is a pretty good one," Joannie acknowledged. "The next day, he blew me off."

"I was an asshole back then," Jonathan said.

"Back then?" Julia shot back.

Joannie realized that she was cold. She slid on the sweatpants and sweatshirt. Now they were all wearing the same clothes.

Johnny had also brought out a bottle of whiskey and a bag of potato chips. He sat at the table and began pouring drinks. Julia hadn't changed, putting on a gray sweatshirt over her evening gown. She walked over to the table and sat next to Johnny. The man who was not her husband. She leaned her shoulder against his. It was a bold move. Strange.

"Do you remember?" Julia said. "Back in the seventies, how our parents used to have key parties?"

"What?" Johnny said. "Maybe *your* parents did."

But Joannie, she remembered.

She remembered going to parties and not being able to find her parents. One time, she had found one of her mother's best friends kissing the father of one of Joannie's friends in a dark bedroom, her shirt off. Joannie looked at the straps of her mother's friend's bra. Joannie asked if they knew where her mother was and her mother's friend said to try the bathroom, and there Joannie found her mother, throwing up into the toilet. Another man was in there, too, holding back her mother's hair. He was not her father.

"Is Mommy throwing up?" she asked.

"Just a little bit," the man responded.

"We'll go home soon, sweetheart," her mother said, not looking up. "Go back to the party and I'll find you."

Joannie had been confused, but relieved to find her mother, and she dutifully went back outside and joined the kids on the swing set. She didn't understand until years later what she had seen. Where was her father? Hadn't he also come to the party?

"I remember," Joannie said.

There had been all sorts of inappropriate behavior in her parents' circle of friends. Her mother had had affairs. Her father had, too. And then at a certain point, all that drama had stopped.

It was different for Joannie. Her marriage. She had spent the first years of Lucy's life basically obsessed with her daughter, concerned only about Lucy's happiness. Probably at the expense of her own, but not really, because making Lucy happy made Joannie happy. She had been terrified that she was going to fuck up being a mother. She did not want to be the kind of mother who was having sex with someone else's husband while her child wandered around a party lost and sad.

Anyway, if Joannie had had needs, she wasn't even aware of them. They did not matter. She got out of her marriage, in part, so that she could stop having sex with her husband. And then years went by. She knew from books and TV that sex was something that was supposed to matter. Some of the parents in her old neighborhood had divorced, and some of them, like Joannie's parents, had stayed married. There had been no cheating or any specific scandalous thing in Joannie's marriage. She and her husband had been faithful until Joannie couldn't bear it any longer.

"My parents went through a phase, too," Joannie said. "Maybe not key parties, exactly, but the same idea. Everybody was fucking everybody. Monogamy was considered very uncool."

"What are you getting at?" Jonathan asked his wife.

"I think we have an opportunity here," Julia said.

She picked up her glass of whiskey, swirled the brown liquid around, and then emptied most of the glass in one swallow. Joannie looked at Julia, and her heart started beating faster.

"It's our anniversary," Jonathan said, putting his hand on top of Julia's. Julia's shoulder was still touching Johnny's. Johnny could have moved away, but he did not.

"This is what I would like to do," Julia said. "For our anniversary. The hot air balloon was not a big success, as you know. You and Joannie, it seems, have some unfinished business."

"You want to swing?" Joannie asked. She had absolutely no interest in having sex with Jonathan Foster. "Was that what it was called? Swinging?"

Julia shrugged.

"Your parents were swingers," Johnny said.

Joannie nodded. "I guess so." She hadn't thought of them that way, but later, there had been a movie about the phenomenon. People had key parties. There was not that kind of organization in her parents' neighborhood.

"Joannie and I are on a date," Johnny said to Julia. Joannie had thought he had forgotten. She watched as he opened the bag of potato chips.

"Could be fun," Julia said. She was talking, clearly, to Johnny, ignoring her husband. "Have you been seeing each other a long time?" Julia asked.

"It's our first date," Johnny said.

Julia grinned.

"There's some room for exploration, I think."

Joannie looked at Johnny. She had known from that first kiss that she did not want to take it any further, but she also had liked him. She still did. And now that she had swum in his pool, she wondered if she might want to try kissing him again. The date, however, had been taken over, hijacked by the hot air balloon, and while Joannie might have been interested in Julia, it was clear that this feeling was not mutual. And now that Julia was interested in Johnny, Joannie felt herself reconsidering, wondering if it was not his fault or the kiss itself, but the fact that she was out of practice. Tonight, she realized, was an opportunity. She *was* out of practice.

Julia lifted her whiskey glass.

"Salut," she said.

The four adults clinked glasses.

Joannie started to laugh. The whiskey was good, too.

Why not? she thought.

⟶

Joannie and Johnny went to go check on the kids one last time. Lucy was in a pair of striped blue boys' pajamas. She and Tyson were still in the basement playroom straight out of a Pottery

Barn Kids catalogue, and they were lying in sleeping bags on top of the pullout couch because Tyson thought sleeping bags were more official than sheets and blankets.

"You okay?" Joannie asked her daughter, kissing the top of her head.

She realized that she was a little bit drunk. The way her mother had been drunk at that party. Joannie always worried that she would end up being like her mother, as hard as she fought against it. Now this, she thought. It had never occurred to Joannie that she would be in a situation like this. Had she agreed to switch partners? She did not even have a partner.

"You smell funny," Lucy said.

Joannie knew that this must be true. She did not know if it was the whiskey, the wine, or maybe the chlorine from the swimming pool.

"I went swimming," Joannie said.

"Your mom is a good swimmer," Johnny said.

"I know," Lucy said. "I want to go swimming. That's not fair."

"It's late," Joannie said. "We are all in our pajamas."

"You are sleeping over, too, right?"

"Right," Joannie said. "Tyson lives in a very big house, and there are bedrooms for all of us."

"This is fun," Lucy said.

"It *is* fun. A big sleepover party."

"Can I sleep with you?" Lucy asked.

"Well." Joannie stalled. She wasn't really sure about what was going to happen next. "The grown-ups are going to stay up for a while. You'll be asleep by the time we go to bed. It's better you stay with Tyson. But I will check on you."

"I want to stay up late," Tyson said, yawning. He was practically asleep.

"We'll both check on you," Johnny said.

"Mom," Lucy said. She looked worried. She looked overtired. Maybe she had already changed her mind. She slept with Joannie most nights. Every night, really.

"It's time for bed, kiddos," Johnny said. "I'm making pancakes in the morning. Do you like bacon?"

Joannie could see Lucy's mind quickly change back into sleepover mode.

"I love bacon. I want to eat all the bacon. I can eat six pieces of bacon," she said.

"It's true," Joannie agreed.

Johnny got down on his knees and kissed Lucy and then his son on the top of the head.

Joannie did the same thing, though she felt strange kissing Tyson. He did not seem like an unpleasant child. Again, she was getting ahead of herself. He would not be her stepson.

"You aren't sleeping with Tyson's dad, are you?" Lucy asked.

Joannie shook her head. "No," she said. "Of course not. I'll be in the room next to his."

This, of course, was true. The plan, apparently, was that she would be sleeping with Jonathan. Joannie was not sure if she had actually agreed to that.

In the morning, Joannie thought, she would show Lucy the hot air balloon in the pool. They could dive down in the pool, try to sit in the submerged basket. The morning felt like a very long time away. She wondered how her parents could have done the things they had done. Would she?

"Good night, sweet pea," she said. "Good night, Tyson."

Tyson, she thought, was a weird name. It made her think of fried chicken.

Johnny squeezed her hand, and they walked upstairs together. At the block party the night they met, he had told her that *My Life as a Dog* had been his favorite movie when he was a teenager. It had made him love movies. Foreign films. It had changed him. It had been Joannie's favorite movie, too, when she was seventeen and figuring out what kind of person she wanted to be. She had seen it three times, and every time, the movie made her cry. This had felt important, somehow.

"Wild night," Johnny said, grinning.

Johnny really seemed to be enjoying himself.

Joannie, of course, didn't know him at all.

You could not love a person just because you had the same favorite movie as a teenager.

What about us? she wanted to ask him, despite the fact that she did not want an "us." But she would have loved to live in this house. There was that.

Joannie found herself in a bedroom with Jonathan.

It was a very pleasant bedroom. Johnny was an architect. He had good taste in books and furniture. It was nice to know, even if Joannie had not been attracted to him, that he at least had been attracted to her. That had to count for something. For her future. Joannie genuinely believed that she had stopped being attractive to men. She wasn't thin the way she used to be. She did not wax her pubic hair or wear nice underwear. She wore oversize clothes. On Facebook, Joannie had noticed that many of her college girlfriends who had gotten married and divorced had then turned gay, and Joannie wondered if that could be a possibility for her, too. Joannie worried that she was not good-looking enough for the good-looking lesbians either. Unattractive to men and women. Julia, for instance, wasn't interested. But Jonathan had not objected vigorously when Julia had suggested the partner swap. He was hurt about the anniversary, but also amenable to the idea of Joannie.

There they were in a room together, wearing matching sweats. Joannie watched as Jonathan took off his sweatshirt. Fortunately, he was wearing a white T-shirt underneath. Johnny must have lent him that, too. She had thought he was cute when he was fourteen. She had told another girl at camp about her kiss with Jonathan and the girl had not believed her.

Anyway, she was not ugly. Joannie had just lost confidence in herself. Maybe this night could be good for her confidence.

⟋

They sat down next to each other, side by side, on the bed.

"How many years has it been?" he asked.

At first she thought he was asking her how long it had been since she'd had sex, but he just meant since they had met.

Joannie was too drunk and too tired to do the math.

"It was before high school."

"I always thought you were pretty."

"Just not pretty enough," Joannie said. She was surprised by how much she remembered. Really, if she was going to have sex with Jonathan Foster, it would be better if they didn't talk.

"I wasn't really surprised," she said. "I was not going to be one of the popular kids. Honestly, I was surprised you noticed me the first night. I was ridiculously happy that you chose me."

It was true.

Joannie had not spent over twenty years feeling hurt by a minor rejection, but it was possible that this early rejection had informed her view of herself. This realization made Joannie sad. She had been in therapy after her divorce, and she had loved it, but the sessions were expensive, and she had stopped during the pandemic. With Lucy home, it was too difficult to have sessions, talking on the phone in the bathroom. Lucy always wanted to know who she was talking to. Or wanted to go to the bathroom.

"Man, that's embarrassing," Jonathan said.

"It was my first kiss," Joannie said.

"Oh shit," Jonathan said. "I'm sorry."

Joannie shrugged. "It was another lifetime."

It wasn't. It was the same lifetime. Joannie, however, did not want Jonathan to believe that she cared. That he had somehow wounded her.

"My wife wants to cheat on me in the next room," Jonathan said. "She really hates me. I did not know how much until tonight. I thought we were good."

Joannie did not have an answer for that. His wife could, in fact, be cheating on him at that moment. She probably was.

Life was strange.

Outside, exhilarated from her swim in the cold water, from saving this man's life, a drink in hand, she had thought, *Why not?* Now, sitting in a bedroom with Jonathan Foster, the door closed, Joannie knew that she wouldn't be able to go through with it. It wasn't a moral thing, even though she had been judgmental of her parents' behavior. It was more like clarity.

"Julia used to love me," Jonathan said. He would not stop talking. "I ruined everything. And it isn't just the sex with other women. It is how I spend my money. Supporting political candidates. And not always the good ones. Julia is the philanthropist in the marriage. I thought we balanced each other out."

"Okay," Joannie said.

She would not have sympathy for a rich man's regret about how he spent his money.

"And then there was the trouble getting pregnant."

"Oh," Joannie said, the best she could do.

"You get to this point where you realize that your money isn't bringing you pleasure. And I love money. I keep on making more of it. I've come out of this pandemic richer than ever."

"Oh my God," Joannie said. "Seriously. I don't want to hear that."

Joannie rubbed her eyes. She couldn't go home now. She had told Lucy that she would stay, and her daughter was probably asleep. It would be good for Lucy to have a sleepover. She had been deprived of other kids for so long.

"If I had money," Joannie said, "it would make me happy."

"You think so?"

Jonathan looked at her.

"I would buy a house. I would get better food at the supermarket. I would buy organic raspberries. I would not use the money for evil."

"Do you really think she is fucking him?" Jonathan asked.

Joannie realized that Jonathan wasn't listening to her. "It seems likely," she said. "This was all her idea."

This was Julia's way, almost literally, of sticking it to him. Though that wasn't exactly right. It was being stuck to her. Johnny, clearly, was up for things in a way that Joannie was not. Life, to him, was a party.

He might still want a second date, after fucking Julia.

Joannie lay back on the bed.

She could ask Julia how it was.

The day was catching up to her.

Jonathan lay back on the bed next to her. He put his hand on hers. He leaned over and tried to kiss her. Joannie pushed him away.

"Let's go to sleep," Joannie said.

"Are you sure?" Jonathan said. "I sort of owe you a second kiss. Let me rephrase that. I want to kiss you."

Joannie had gotten herself into the situation.

It was just sex. Physical. He was not unattractive. Joannie could kiss him and see if she was still able to breathe. This, unfortunately, made Joannie remember that they were still living in a pandemic. She was vaccinated, but still, she did not need to be kissing a man she did not even like. It would not be a successful experiment.

At that moment, Lucy tentatively opened the door and, seeing her mother, ran into the room. She was so ridiculously cute in Tyson's blue-and-white-striped pajamas, solving the problem for Joannie.

"Mommy," Lucy said. "I can't sleep."

"Oh, sweetie," Joannie said. "That's okay."

She was so happy to see her beautiful daughter. She loved this little girl so much. Joannie patted the bed.

"Come sleep with me."

Lucy hopped up on the bed and got under the covers.

"Who is that man?" she asked her mother.

"That is Jonathan Foster," Joannie said. "There weren't enough bedrooms for everyone. But he is leaving. He can sleep on the couch. That would be better for everyone."

"Sleep well," Jonathan said, taking his cue.

He smiled at Joannie.

"I hope you get your house one day," he said to her.

He *had* been listening.

Jonathan got off the bed and closed the door behind him. Joannie did not know how her parents had done it, having all that sex with the neighbors. Joannie got under the covers, next to her little girl. She spooned her body around her. She kissed the back of Lucy's head. Johnny had promised pancakes and bacon for breakfast. She assumed that he would make good coffee. Joannie closed her eyes.

It was a comfortable bed.

Johnny

Julia Foster was a famous philanthropist. It had always seemed calculated to Johnny. Her job was to give away money to redeem her husband. For the most part, it had worked.

Johnny wondered, if he made her come, what cause could he ask her to contribute to? His mind went blank. Something she had overlooked. The water in Mississippi. Or Michigan. Then, of course, he knew. The public housing project he wanted to build in town. There was so much bloody politics, though, and while he knew the right people, they liked the idea but didn't want to hire him. Johnny had trouble understanding this. His design was so good. The idea of it made him hard.

Still, it was difficult for Johnny to concentrate, having sex with one of the most famous philanthropists in the country. She was giving money to nurses. Out-of-work actors. Waiters. Farmers. The Black Lives Matter movement. Anyone who had proved hardship during the pandemic. He had seen her on television. She was a genuinely good person, and this was what he was doing? Fucking her? Julia had pretty breasts, but Johnny found himself wondering about Joannie. About Joannie's breasts. How they would compare. He had blown his chances with her, and he had liked her, but come on. A hot air balloon in his backyard. A beautiful woman literally asking to come into his bed. No games, no foreplay. It had been awhile. Dating was so much work. How could he say no?

"Focus," Julia told him.

It was true, he had lost focus. Johnny was overstimulated. Thinking instead of feeling. He was hard, but he couldn't come, and according to his former wife, that was the very worst thing for a woman, having sex with a man who couldn't come. The endless panting, pretending. It was like a form of rape, she once told him during couples counseling, which he had found wildly offensive. How could having consensual sex with his wife be rape? It was such bullshit. It made Johnny angry every time he remembered it. Now this thought made his penis go completely limp.

Johnny slid off Julia, dispirited, furious with himself, but fortunately, she saved the situation. Julia pushed his head between her legs. She put her fingers in his hair and pressed his face down. No words, but the instructions were clear.

"Oh," Johnny said.

Long before the divorce, his wife had stopped letting

him go there. After their marriage, she decided she was gay. Still, they remained friends. Everything made more sense to Johnny. None of it was his fault; the fact that she found him repulsive was because she did not like men. It was not about him. This was strangely helpful.

"You taste delicious," Johnny told Julia.

"Don't talk," she said. Her eyes were closed. "More pressure," she said. She really seemed determined.

And so Johnny licked harder. And slid a finger into her pussy and licked and touched and she writhed and it was the most amazing thing, to watch her come. Julia gasped and moaned. She caught her breath. She even blushed, after she came. Her face had turned rosy.

"My husband doesn't do that to me anymore," she said.

"You're amazing," he told her.

And she shook her head. Johnny wanted to tell her he loved her, but he knew that he was stupid that way. He always fell in love. Johnny put Julia's hand on his cock, but she did not take hold of it. She turned on her side and fell asleep.

Fair enough, he thought.

⟋

Johnny woke up early, Julia asleep in his bed.

He felt rather pleased with himself.

He dressed and went downstairs to the kitchen, wondering what he would find. He passed Jonathan Foster twisted on the couch, barely covered by a white throw, his legs bare. The throw pillows on the floor. He, obviously, had not gotten so lucky. Johnny remembered then that it was this man's wife he had been with. He should have felt remorse, but then he realized that he did not have to. They had made a deal. He wished Joannie had kept her end of the bargain, because it did not seem fair, and then he remembered the voice of his wife, explaining how he had raped her for years. Joannie was entitled to whatever choice she wanted to make.

Johnny and Fern had been divorced for five years, and he still had not gotten her voice out of his head.

Joannie and her daughter, Lucy, were in the kitchen. Lucy was kneeling on her chair, eating an apple. Joannie was pouring herself a cup of coffee. They had settled in.

"I made a pot," she said. "I hope that's okay."

"Of course, of course," he said. "Thank you."

Johnny had the impulse to kiss her good morning, but Joannie stepped away. This made sense, but it still stung. He had not expected another woman to drop from the sky. He could still be blamed for his actions, however. That's what Fern would say.

Lucy was staring at him, the expression on her face strangely expectant. He hoped that she did not think he was going to be her new daddy. He hated to let children down. Tyson was constantly disappointed with him. The last time they went out to do something together—play tennis—Tyson had lain down on the court, refusing to move. This had mystified Johnny. It had been Tyson's idea to play.

"What is it?" Johnny asked Lucy. He hated it when women were displeased with him. It was no different, he realized, with a little girl.

"You promised bacon."

"Bacon!" Johnny's voice was too loud. He made an effort to tone it down. "I promised bacon. I will make the bacon."

He wanted it to sound like "Time to make the donuts," like the TV commercial, but Joannie did not smile at his joke.

"Bacon!" Lucy, at least, was beaming. That was better.

Johnny opened the refrigerator.

"Oh no," he said. "We are all out of bacon."

"Oh," Lucy said. Her face immediately fell. "You promised."

"You promised," Joannie said. Her voice was also sad, but she did not seem surprised.

"I was kidding," Johnny said. "Kidding. I was kidding. I have bacon. I'll make the bacon right now."

"You were teasing me," Lucy said.

Johnny realized that, as fast as that, he had lost her. Which meant that he had lost Joannie, too. Joannie looked adorable, wearing a white T-shirt and sweatpants. Everyone looked so different in the morning, without their makeup, without their hair brushed. In the clothes they had slept in. There was sort of a purity to it. He had been so pleased when she had said yes to the date. She had required convincing. That was why he'd had her and Lucy over to his house. She would not go to a restaurant, even though people were going to eat at restaurants and it was warm enough to eat outside. Harder to get around was the fact that she would not leave Joannie with a babysitter. Johnny was pleased with himself when he came up with a workaround.

Julia, he realized, was not going to help with his housing project idea. She was going to eat breakfast and go back to whatever wealthy enclave from which she came. How, Johnny was not sure, since the hot air balloon in which she and Jonathan had arrived was at the bottom of the pool. Johnny looked out the window. There was the pool, a crystal-clear blue, and there was the hot air balloon. It looked like it was a beautiful day. A beautiful spring day. He could drive them home, spare them the cost of an Uber. He would be happy to do that. They were, of course, insanely wealthy. It was surprising, really, that they had stayed as long as they had. Then Johnny remembered that it was the weekend.

Johnny would offer them a ride. He wanted to see their home. Fern had never thought she and Johnny were rich enough; she envied so many of their neighbors with their bigger houses. When it came time to divorce, she moved out of their house and bought the house across the street. It was so easy, sending Tyson back and forth. Sometimes Johnny did not even walk the boy over. He could watch from the living room window as Tyson crossed the street, wheeling a little suitcase. It could be painful, still, to see his ex-wife, the woman who did not want to be with him. Johnny wondered if she had seen the hot air balloon plummet. But if she had, she would have shown up, right away.

He had made Julia Foster come.

He looked at Joannie, pouring cream into her coffee, and thought of Julia, asleep in his bed. She would go back to wherever she came from. Joannie was real. His hand brushed hers as he got his coffee.

Again, she moved away.

"I noticed Jonathan on the couch," Johnny said. He drank

the coffee she'd made. He opened the package of bacon. He had better not fuck around.

"Lucy woke up," Joannie said. "So."

He understood. He felt slightly guilty that the partner swap had been one-sided. Of course she would feel affronted.

"How was your night?" she asked.

"A gentleman does not kiss and tell," Johnny said, which he realized was the equivalent of telling. He could not help it. He felt so good. And he would provide Lucy with delicious bacon. He could change her mind about him.

"Where's Tyson?" Johnny asked.

"He's still sleeping," Joannie said. "We checked."

"Go wake him up," Johnny told Lucy. "Jump on the bed. Tell him I am making breakfast. Bring him back with you."

"I can jump on the bed?" Lucy asked.

Johnny looked at Joannie. She shrugged.

"You can jump on the bed," Johnny said. "Wake up Tyson. And then pancakes and bacon."

Lucy looked at Johnny as if he was crazy, and then she ran to the basement. Johnny and Joannie were alone in the kitchen.

"I want to say . . . ," Johnny said, not sure of what he wanted to say but wanting to say something. Joannie shook her head.

"Let's just not say anything," she said.

"But—"

"I can get started on the pancakes," she said. "If you want some help."

"I've got it covered," Johnny said. "You relax."

He got the ingredients for pancakes. Flour, eggs, vegetable oil. Mini chocolate chips. He would cut up fresh strawberries.

The dad thing had always been easier than the husband or boyfriend game. Life was always a little bit inscrutable. Why, for instance, wasn't Joannie happy, beaming with good energy, the promise of another day? He almost wanted to tell her to go home, leave her daughter, take the day for herself. Just go. Women were always, always such hard work.

Julia

Julia hadn't always wanted children.

She had decided when she was a teenager that she didn't want kids and then had never questioned that decision. She had had a dream, though, where she was a mother, and she had an adorable child, a little girl with wispy hair, looking at her with adoration, and she thought this dream meant something. The meaning of this dream could not be more obvious, and when she told Jonathan, he said, "Let's do it." And they got married. They were both thirty-eight. They planned the wedding for a day that Julia was ovulating, hoping for immediate conception. Julia thought that one day she could tell her future child that she'd been created on her parents' wedding day. But while Julia and Jonathan were both lucky people, they were not that lucky.

She could not get pregnant.

And they tried.

The old-fashioned way.

And then the IVF way.

This was what they did, during quarantine. They focused on making that baby happen. It turned out that Julia's eggs were not viable. Julia did not want an egg donor. She did not want to raise a baby that was half Jonathan, no Julia. She was open to adopting, keen on the idea of a Vietnamese baby. Vivian, Jonathan's personal assistant, was adopted. From Vietnam. And Vivian was wonderful, and Julia knew that that was where she had gotten the idea, but it was still a good idea. For her future daughter to turn out like Vivian. But Jonathan did not want to raise a child that was not biologically his. He was adamant. This made no sense to her, and the hypocrisy was galling since he was okay with the idea that she have a child that was not biologically hers. But no matter how hard they tried to come up with a plan, this was something upon which they could not agree. Jonathan refused to raise a child of unknown parentage.

"We have too many nice things," he said, "to risk it all."

This made, she kept saying, no sense.

Their own biological child, for instance, could also be a total nightmare. That sometimes happened. There was never a guarantee. Their own biological child could turn out to be the spawn of the devil. They could not agree. They did not even fight, which felt worse to Julia, but she could not win a fight with Jonathan. He would get smug and that infuriated her. She had once gotten so enraged with smug Jonathan that she started hitting him, and eventually he hit her back. It was, in his defense, self-defense. Julia would not fight with him again. She could not always control her anger. Vivian saw the black eye the next day and said nothing. She gave Julia a much-needed hug. It had been mortifying. Julia assumed the divorce was coming. No baby, no marriage. What was the point? The last few months, especially, it had felt like a game of chicken. Who would make the first move?

She had done it last night. It felt good.

Julia was going to end it. She only had to figure out when and how. Be judicious. Her life was very comfortable, and sometimes she thought, *Why bother?* Stay the course. Live a pleasant life. The reason to came to light when Jonathan began to publicly humiliate her. He was taking supermodels and actresses to the galas she refused to go to. And then to five-star hotels. Restaurants. It was not her imagination. His infidelities were posted on the Internet.

Jonathan was forty-three and his sperm was just fine. It was just a matter of time before he found a different woman.

Not this woman, at least. Joannie. She already had a beautiful daughter. She might fall for his bullshit. Most people did.

⟶

Maybe that was why she had suggested the partner swap.

She had also been pissed. The whole fucking hot air balloon debacle. Apparently, Jonathan had taken lessons but had not counted on the wind. Julia did not understand why he would go through the effort to put on such a big show for their anniversary. He was going big, trying to win her back.

Failing.

Johnny, not surprisingly, turned out to be a mistake. He was basically a friendly oaf. She was not attracted to him. Julia masturbated regularly, but it had been nice to have another person touch her. She closed her eyes and thought about Jeremy Irons, the British actor. She loved his accent.

It was the smell of bacon that lured her from bed.

At the kitchen table, there were two children eating bacon.

A little boy. Blond, loud. Unappealing.

And a little girl. Quiet. Probably unable to talk because her mouth was full of food. Enormously appealing. This was the little girl of Julia's heart. The child she would have wanted to have. She reminded her of the girl in her dream. The wispy hair. Big brown eyes. Julia only wanted to have a girl. She only wanted to have a smart, pretty girl. The girl was missing her two front teeth. She wore a headband with cat ears.

"Who are you?" Julia asked.

"I am Lucy," Lucy said. "Who are you?"

"I'm Julia."

"We had a big sleepover last night," Lucy said. "Everybody was sleeping with everybody."

"I know," Julia said. "I slept over, too."

"You did?" Lucy asked. "I didn't see you."

"I was here!" Julia said with fake enthusiasm. "You were already asleep when we came."

Julia nodded at Joannie, who was also sitting at the table with the children, drinking coffee. She had a notebook open. She had made a small drawing of the flowers on the table. And of her coffee cup. They were good drawings. Julia, of course, also drew. Julia had gone to art school. She used to paint portraits. Landscapes, too. She had stopped a long time ago. She used to make money, selling her art, but it felt like too much trouble. The whole it's-who-you-know game to get gallery exhibits. The demand to make her work big when she liked to paint small.

Somehow, she had married an incredibly wealthy man. A titan in his industry. He worked all the time; she no longer felt the need to make money. It seemed silly, given how little she earned. Diluted the pleasure she used to feel. Sometimes she painted, but sadly it never was the same. Mainly, she gave Jonathan's money away. They had created a foundation, the Foster Foundation—his name, but it was all her, selecting causes, researching foundations, making phone calls, conducting interviews. Transferring enormous sums of money. She thought it would make her feel good about herself, but it didn't always. There were times when she was filled with fury. She would donate money first and then read the fine print later. Often, charities were in fact iffy foundations, with directors and administrators who commanded large salaries and spent their donations not on the cause itself but on gifts during fundraising campaigns. It did not help the polar bears to print expensive calendars.

Jonathan, of course, kept on working like an obsessive lunatic. Money had no value to him. She was surprised that he'd agreed to even stay over. Wherever they were. Not making money. She still held some power over him. She had not thought marriage would be this difficult.

"I slept with Mommy," Lucy said.

Julia nodded, taking in the information. Julia was glad that her husband had not gotten any. Everything always came too easy for him. She didn't think Joannie—an inferior version of herself—would be his type, though honestly, she hadn't really given that any consideration the night before. She had been angry.

Julia hated being angry. Carrying so much hatred in her heart. She felt as if toxicity emanated from her skin, that she was radioactive. She could do something like meditate or practice yoga, but the moment she sat still, the angry thoughts flooded her brain. She could not sit silently with her thoughts. Recently, because Jonathan kept insisting, she had gone to a psychiatrist. She did not see a therapist, his first suggestion, because she was not interested in actual therapy. She did not want to talk and talk about her problems. If she was going to have to face herself, she wanted pills. Anxiety pills. Sleeping pills. She had been surprised by the diagnosis she had received instead. ADHD. She had been prescribed better pills than she had ever hoped for. Essentially speed. Her mind was clear, focused, and she felt better. Most of the time.

"Good morning," Julia said to Joannie.

She smiled. It was a real smile, friendly, warm. While she had no interest in Johnny, the orgasm had been real. Maybe, Julia realized, as if a lightbulb had gone on in her head, at that particular moment in time, she wasn't angry. She was in a new kitchen with new people and she did not hate them. She was not in a hurry to leave. It felt strange.

She wondered if she would have felt differently if Joannie had slept with Jonathan. She had not been surprised to hear that Jonathan had been a prick when he was a teenager. He deserved a little rejection for a change.

Joannie smiled at Julia. It was a shy smile. Less direct than her daughter's. She had a piece of her hair in her mouth, probably a nervous habit, one that she might not even be aware of. There was a plate in front of her, a pile of cold pancakes, a pool of maple syrup, a half-eaten piece of bacon.

"Looks like I'm late for breakfast," Julia said.

"Not at all, not at all." Johnny was at the stove, wearing an apron, hard at work. "There is more bacon in the oven and pancakes on the griddle. A new pot of coffee brewing. You have, in fact, excellent timing."

All of these things were true. Julia experienced a flash of regret.

"Good morning, sweetheart," Johnny said.

She heard it. Joannie heard it. The familiarity. Unearned. It was not okay for him to call her sweetheart. Julia wondered, then, if Joannie might actually *like* Johnny. Suddenly, she felt like an asshole. She had always been slow to consider other people's feelings. Her mother had once told Julia that she was a cold and unfeeling girl. This was when Julia was in high school. It was more than twenty years later, and Julia had never forgiven her. She had gotten over it, sent her mother Christmas presents and birthday presents, still visited her on holidays, but she had never forgotten it. Julia poured herself a cup of coffee and sat down next to Lucy.

"What grade are you in?" she asked the little girl.

"Third."

"And you like cats," Julia said.

"How did you know?"

Julia pointed at the cat ears.

"I love cats," Lucy said. "I can't have any, though, because our landlord won't let us."

"Oh no," Julia said. "You must move!"

"I'm looking for a new place," Joannie said, joining the conversation. She kept on drawing, not looking up.

"You always say that," Lucy said.

Julia recognized a conversation that had been had before. The subject of moving. She did not want to cause any more trouble. She wanted Lucy to have cats.

"I'm trying," Joannie said, making eye contact with Julia and then looking away. "We have a good deal on our apartment," she said. "I can't find anything comparable."

"But no cats," Lucy said. "So it's a bad deal."

"You should come to my house," Julia said. "I have six cats. And I have another dozen cats that I feed and take care of."

Wow, Julia thought, she was being a total bitch. Bragging about her cats. But it was true, about the cats. Most people did not envy her her cats. Most people did not even know about them.

"Six cats!" Lucy said. "I'm so jealous."

Julia had earned the girl's respect. Maybe even her adoration. It felt so good, the way Lucy looked at her. This was how, she had hoped, her daughter would have looked at her. If Julia had a child of her own, she would never say unnecessarily cruel things to her, scarring her for life. When the doctor told her she had ADHD, it had come as such a relief. Not just because of the very good pills, but because of the validation. She was different. Her brain was different. And no one, especially her mother, had ever understood her. Sometimes she thought Jonathan got her. And this was not a small thing. There were reasons they stayed together.

"We are cat people," Julia said. "You should come see my cats."

"Okay," Lucy said. "I want to. Today?"

"Maybe." Julia drank her coffee. She closed her eyes. She had no idea what was in her calendar. She had let her phone die. It was charging now. Jonathan was asleep on the sofa. It was as if the hot air balloon crash had shifted something in their brains that even the pandemic had failed to. They had slowed down. Had they had a near-death experience? She wondered how far from home they had drifted. "Today could possibly work."

"Well," Joannie said.

Possibly was not a useful word when it came to making plans with children.

"I want to come!" the little boy said. "I want to see the cats."

Julia had already forgotten about the little boy sitting at the table. She had tuned him out entirely. She had absolutely no interest in him. She had wondered, when she was trying to get pregnant, what would happen if she had a boy. A friend had told her that she would fall instantly in love and she would be fine. Julia had not been convinced, but she had never had to find out.

This was another reason to divorce Jonathan. Because

without him, she could go ahead and adopt her own Vietnamese baby. A girl. The idea occurred to her while she was sitting in Johnny's kitchen, like a flash of lightning. Jonathan was getting in the way of her having a child. It was a big realization, an obvious one, one she was surprised that she had not had before. Maybe she had wanted her marriage to work and so she had made compromises, bad decisions, agreed to things she should not have. It was over, though. The marriage. She had proven that the night before. Somehow, this made Julia nervous. Her leg started to shake.

"You don't like cats, Ty," Johnny said from the stove.

"You don't like cats?" Lucy asked.

"I got scratched by a cat once," Tyson explained.

"I get scratched by my cats all the time," Julia said. She was putting the kid down, and she knew it. It helped her, somehow, to be rude to this child. Steadied her. "I still love them."

"I have a dog," Tyson said.

"No one asked you," Julia responded. "We are talking about cats."

Julia saw the boy's face fall. She saw the surprise on Joannie's face, too. Clearly she had messed up, stepped out of line, talking to him the way she had, enjoying it. Julia had not spent much time around children. She was doing fine with Lucy, though.

"Where is your dog?" Lucy asked. "I haven't seen a dog. Are you lying?"

"I'm not lying," Tyson said. "She's at my mom's house across the street. I'll go get her."

He jumped up from his chair.

"Don't get the dog, son," Johnny said.

Julia looked at him, as if for the first time. In the bright light of the morning sun. He was not bad-looking. He was actually similar to her husband, but less handsome. She had used this man. That was the first time she had ever done something like that, but he had not seemed to mind. The expression on his face, now, looking at her, was hopeful, but there was no hope. They weren't going there again. It was at that moment that Jonathan entered the room. He looked hungover. Still, he noticed Julia and Johnny looking at each other. Julia noticed him noticing. She willed her leg to stop shaking.

This was another thing Julia had not considered. The morning after. Breakfast. The four of them in a room together. It was all slightly ridiculous. Entertaining, even. Somehow, Julia wasn't hungover. Julia felt great, really. She was going to show this little girl her cats. She loved showing off her cats. Most of the time, people did not care. In the past, she had been mocked for donating money to cat sanctuaries.

"I like your drawings," she said to Joannie.

Joannie blushed. Joannie, she understood, would be easy to manipulate. Maybe Julia could help her find a new apartment. Julia had an obscene amount of money, but it was often strangely hard to help people. They had pride, dignity, bullshit issues that made it difficult for her to share her wealth. This had happened before. If she said, right then, *Here's a hundred thousand dollars, go find a new apartment,* what would this woman do? Julia was tempted to do it. Just to see.

Johnny came over to the table, carrying a plate filled with pancakes and bacon in one hand and a pot of coffee in the other. He put the food down and refilled her cup. He put his hand on her shoulder. In front of Jonathan. It was a dumb move. Unnecessary. Unwanted.

"Eat," he said. "Have a seat," he said to Jonathan. "I'll grab you a mug."

Last night, Johnny going down on her, that had been a sign. There was pleasure to be had outside of Jonathan. He could no longer bring her any kind of pleasure. Once she'd realized that Jonathan could not give her a baby, she had even started to dislike and then hate him. It was not his fault. It was her body's, but it was easier to hate him. She looked at him, standing awkwardly at the table, not sure if he wanted to sit down, and she felt her hate for him rise up like vomit.

She turned her attention back to Joannie. She needed a haircut. Her nails were uneven. She was meek. Not unappealing. But not like her daughter. Oh my God, her daughter. That beautiful little girl. Her daughter loved cats. This was going to be Julia's in. She could feel it.

She had a feeling, too, that Joannie could use a break, another pool. Why not? Jonathan and Julia had a gorgeous pool. They rarely used it. Julia thought swimming was a waste of time. Sometimes Jonathan remarked on the fact that they did not enjoy their good fortune. That it was wasted on them. Jonathan would feel good, having Joannie and Lucy swim in their pool. It would justify the cost, though really, money had no value, so she was surprised, sometimes, that he cared.

Jonathan

The scene at the breakfast table was hell.

Jonathan was not able to play along.

He said his good mornings, took his cup of coffee and three pieces of bacon on a napkin, and went outside to stare at the hot air balloon sitting upright in the bottom of the pool. That had happened.

Idiot.

Jonathan had more money than ever. He was a verified billionaire, according to Vivian, his personal assistant, who had recently hired a publicist to work on his public image. He had no business flying a hot air balloon over a residential area, but somehow, he was able to do things that other people could not. The hot air balloon people had advised him, had given him specific instructions about problems he might encounter, and he had nodded. "I know, I know," he'd said, as if they were fucking morons, and he and Julia had set off. A new adventure. He had taken lessons.

Now he took a photo of the hot air balloon at the bottom of the pool and sent it to Vivian in a text message.

"Here's a challenge for you," he wrote.

She could take care of it. She was the one who had actually rented the balloon, after all, set up the lessons. It occurred to him that this was her fault. She should have told him it was a bad idea. He might have listened to her.

He probably wouldn't have.

Vivian was more than an employee to him. He had raised his voice to her only once, when she'd made a small mistake—placed the wrong dinner order—and he'd vowed he never would again. She had actually cried, the sweet thing, and Jonathan had cried, too. He had embraced her; he had laughed. "It's only dinner, Vivvy," he'd said.

Julia had warned him that he was opening himself up to a lawsuit, yelling at an employee, but Vivian wouldn't sue him. Vivian loved him. He knew this, saw it in her eyes. He did not want to hurt her. He did not want to take advantage of her. He never called her Vivvy again. She had been floundering when they met, temping at the office in New York, and now she did everything. Ordered dinners and weighed in on business decisions. She lived with them, had moved into their guesthouse. She shared the dinners she ordered. She had become part of the family.

Julia disagreed. "She gets a paycheck," she said.

Julia was a very cynical person.

The previous night had been such a spectacular failure.

Jonathan was athletic. He had been stunned when he'd lost control of the hot air balloon. The winds had come as a surprise. The instructors had not taught him how to handle the wind. Or had they? Nonetheless, the accident was not his fault. The company had let him take Julia up in the air, not properly trained. He could sue, he was sure of it, though most likely it was not worth his time, the possible bad publicity.

He could hear Julia orgasm from all the way downstairs on the couch. She could have made an effort to be quiet. The orgasm had to have been exaggerated, or flat-out fake, to make him jealous, to make him feel miserable, and it had worked.

This marriage was making him feel miserable.

Julia, he knew, was beginning to give up on the idea of a baby. His solution was a good one. If she did not want a surrogate, she could carry the baby herself. It would have his DNA. She could give birth, breastfeed, have that whole experience. Wasn't that what she wanted?

The truth was, he didn't really want a baby anymore. He'd *thought* he wanted a baby, but then when Julia couldn't have one, he realized that he was not that upset. No baby. Fine. What was he going to do with a Vietnamese orphan? Who was he to take a child from another culture and bring it into his home? The kid would invariably grow up to resent him. It always happened. No matter what, he could never be Asian;

he would not understand what it was like for that child, being forced to assimilate. He would be an asshole. There was no way around it. He could already hear a twenty-year-old screaming at him for ruining her life. No fucking way.

The affairs had started recently. Returning to his single ways had been glorious. Gorgeous women threw themselves at him constantly, and he did not have it in him to turn them down. Not anymore. There were minimal risks. The women he slept with knew that he was married, unavailable. They could try to blackmail him, but Julia knew. The worst these women could do was give him Covid. That was pretty fucking bad, sure, but he was vaccinated. He was healthy. So far he had been lucky.

Joannie was the first person who had turned him down in a very long time. Maybe ever. Had anyone ever turned him down? Maybe it really was because of her little girl. But probably that was an excuse. He could sense her ambivalence but had been fairly confident he would be able to win her over.

Really, it was a good thing that it hadn't happened. Their half of the swap. Because it wouldn't have been casual. Not with her.

Jonathan had a sense, a Spidey sense, of when a woman was going to cling. Joannie would have wanted him. The women he slept with often wanted him, even knowing that he was married, but none of them were single mothers with big sad eyes.

Jonathan's phone buzzed.

Vivian. Amazing as always.

"What the fuck?" she texted.

"Wind."

"Sorry," she wrote. "On it. Do you need a car?"

"Yes," Jonathan wrote back. "I don't know where I am."

He realized that he did not know the address, did not know where he had spent the night, but Vivian texted back with it. "You're here," she wrote.

Jonathan was on Vivian's Find My contacts. It was amazing how often this proved to be useful. Especially since he had started cheating, she had bailed him out several times, located his lost cell phone in airplanes, restaurants, hotel rooms. Basically, she was always saving his ass. Sometimes it was hard to look at her. Wondering what she might think. It was better for him to be fucking other women than thinking about her. He worried she thought about him too often.

Because he would not do that, become involved with her in an inappropriate way. She had to understand that.

She was *his* Vietnamese orphan.

Young enough to be his daughter.

Was he figuring it out just then, waiting for her to rescue him from disaster? Wasn't he supposed to take care of her? He was not. Like Julia said, he gave her a paycheck.

How was it possible that he had such strong feelings for Vivian? His assistant. She was short, only five feet, and Jonathan was tall, six foot two. But she had that pretty, pretty shiny silky hair, and she was so smart. So smart. And so great to talk to. She solved almost any problem he threw at her. The only person smarter than Vivian was Julia, and Vivian did not mock him, not the way Julia did. Jonathan hated to be mocked. Jonathan had been so hopeful, getting married. He had been earnest. He had believed.

He understood that it was his fault, the marriage's decline, but so much had changed after they learned Julia couldn't get pregnant. The sex had become unnecessary. It had stopped being about pleasure, and it felt impossible to get that back. Julia never moaned the way she had last night. She had gone quiet.

Jonathan wondered what Vivian would be like, having sex.

And then, he hated himself.

"You're going to have to tell me the whole story," Vivian texted. Jonathan responded with a winking smiley face. Vivian had taught him about emojis. Vivian, of course, was going to take care of the hot air balloon. She was going to get him home. It made him happy, to picture her face. There was nothing creepy about that. He and Julia had stayed too long. He would talk to her and they would leave. He would forgive her, of course. She had had his permission.

The coffee, at least, was good. Which meant that everything, basically, was fine. If he was going to crash his hot air balloon somewhere, this house wasn't half bad. He could have landed on a highway. They could have been hit by a car. Everything was fine. Except for this Julia sex business. He was not a fan of being fucked with. Fucked over. Julia had to have known, last night, that she was being loud. She had to have known. He was not going to quickly get over this. A divorce was going to cost him, severely cost him, but really, when it was over and done, he would still be wealthy. He also wanted to stay married. He had told Julia this, repeatedly. No baby. It did not matter. That was not why he had fallen for her. He had not realized how much her being with Johnny would bother him.

They had some problems to work out.

He had told her he would stop with the affairs. If she asked him to. He would stop. Because for the most part, they were good together. It was okay, honestly, what had happened last night. He would just have to get used to the idea. Get over it. He did not want to be alone. He did not want to start again, with a new woman. A new woman would want to redecorate his house, be in love. It was so much work. He had done all that with Julia. His friends had expressed surprise when he married her, an artist, an outspoken liberal, a woman his age. But he knew what he was doing.

He looked at the sparkling pool and wondered what kind of chemicals Johnny used. If he should fire his pool company. Sometimes, for no reason, Jonathan got the urge to fire people, hire new ones. Vivian would do it. Sometimes, he felt guilty about giving Vivian unnecessary work. Probably, he should fire her. Through the open window, he heard laughter in the kitchen. *Merriment* was the word that came into his head.

Jonathan sighed.

He felt left out, hearing that laughter.

It was his choice to sit outside, alone, but one of them could have checked on him. Johnny, for instance, who had fucked his wife. He owed him that much. Or Julia, who had fucked Johnny. Or Joannie, even, who had not wanted to fuck him. How relieved she had been when her daughter came into the room, taking his rightful place in the bed. The least she could do was check on him now.

No. They all had somebody, and now they were leaving him alone. Jonathan could not remember the last time he had felt this humiliated. He could not let it stand. He really couldn't.

He would have to woo Joannie, for his self-respect if nothing else. It would not be difficult. She was a single mother. She seemed crazy about that swimming pool. If she wanted to see a beautiful pool, this was nothing.

He would invite Joannie and her daughter to his house. He could take them sailing. Or the girl would like his motorboat. He'd bought it from a buddy, and there was a waterslide attached to the back. This share-your-partner thing, bohemian sexual adventure, whatever the fuck it was, was a challenge, a contest, and he had not lost yet.

Joannie at fourteen was painfully shy. He had kissed her, and he was a good kisser, and even then, he understood how happy she was that he had chosen her. He woke up the next day and he saw better options. It was as simple as that. He used to be an asshole. He was improving. He wanted, at least, to be better.

That was the thing about inappropriate thoughts. They were thoughts. Nothing more.

Jonathan ate the bacon he had brought outside. Amazing, crispy and good. Almost good enough to make him go back inside for more. But he wouldn't. He would stay outside on the beautiful May day and wait. He was not sure who would come first. Men for the hot air balloon. Johnny with a plate of pancakes. He wanted Julia. His wife. It seemed possible that he still loved her. He did not love Vivian, not like that. He loved his wife. He willed her to come. Check on him. Love him. Offer him some pancakes.

Vivian

ere's a challenge for you, Vivian's boss, Jonathan, texted her, as if he was sending a present. Something fun to do. Hooray, a puzzle to solve. She never actually had a day off. He always needed something. Saturday nights, Sundays. Whenever an idea came into his head. Sometimes he sent texts in the middle of the night. Not because he expected Vivian to respond—or at least that was what he said—but because that was when he thought of something. She always read them. She had trouble sleeping.

Jonathan and Julia had not come back from their anniversary date and now it was the next day and Vivian had been worried. She had scoured the Internet, watched the TV news, thought about calling the police or the hot air balloon company, and then realized that unless she was asked to do a specific task, she was not actually responsible for them.

Anyway, there had been nothing on the local news, and a hot air balloon crash would definitely have been reported. Vivian wondered what would happen if Jonathan and Julia Foster died. Would she be held accountable? She had made the arrangements. And then another thought came to her. She was alone in their house. This had not happened once, not during the entire pandemic. She wondered what she could steal. What she would want.

She walked around the house, touching things that she admired. She loved the handblown glass vases from Italy. She wanted the armchairs in the living room, black leather and teakwood, the most comfortable chairs she had ever sat on. There was a rug with a tapestry pattern that looked like it should be in a museum. Vivian loved that rug. She would not take these things. For one thing, Jonathan and Julia would notice. If they were dead, maybe that would change things. It was unlikely the police would notice.

This, she knew, was a strange fantasy to entertain. It was impossible to actually steal anything. She had gotten caught shoplifting at the mall when she was thirteen years old. She had taken a lip gloss—one lip gloss, that was it—and she had been grounded for a month.

Vivian could not steal the view from the house. It was not hers, she did not deserve it. How lovely it was. The beautiful water, the bay. The sunsets and the sunrises. The sounds of the birds in the morning. She could take the very good coffeemaker. It had taken her a while to learn how to use it, but she could make an excellent shot of espresso, which led to cappuccinos, which she found herself drinking all day long. She did not want to imagine life without the coffeemaker, but would she buy one for herself, even though it cost an insane amount of money? She had money saved. Would she let herself do it? Spend that much money on a coffeemaker. Jonathan and Julia would notice if Vivian took the coffeemaker.

More obvious, she could take the ten thousand dollars Jonathan kept in his top desk drawer, extra cash in case he needed to pay the workers. "My father," Jonathan told her, "used to keep cash in the house. For this reason. He had a massage therapist who came to the house once a week."

"Oh," she said, wondering why he told her this. Why he had shown her the money.

Cash had become obsolete.

Jonathan, for instance, never once talked to a worker. Paid a worker. Vivian was responsible for the workers. She was thinking about firing the pool company. The water did not seem to sparkle the way it should.

"It got stolen," Jonathan told her, like he was reminiscing. Like this was an important memory. She never knew when they were coming. "My father's money."

She nodded, waiting for more.

"We never found out who did it," Jonathan said. "Maybe the maid. My mom thought it was this guy named Donny who did odd jobs around the house."

"Who do you think took it?" Vivian asked.

"I think it was my little sister," Jonathan said.

"Your sister?"

"She continues to deny it."

Jonathan never talked to his little sister. Vivian did not know why. It had become her job to send this sister a birthday present. This was a part of her job that she did not like.

"So you still want to keep cash in the house?" she asked him. "Given what you know."

"It makes no sense," Jonathan said. "I know."

Almost everything else Jonathan did made sense. He was allowed this one idiosyncrasy. But it bothered Vivian, the cash in the drawer, because she felt haunted by that money. There were days when she was annoyed with him, with Julia, and she would open the desk drawer and take a hundred dollars. Spend it.

It made her feel good.

And then bad.

She would go to an ATM and get cash, put the money back. It was stupid to steal from the Fosters. She got paid so much. She was saving her money, saving it for grad school. For that coffeemaker she knew she would have to buy. She would not be a personal assistant for the rest of her life, though part of her was very afraid that she would. She would not admit to her friends how much she earned. Not that she had friends. It was alarming how fast she lost touch with everyone when she left Brooklyn. Somehow, they were all keeping on, most of them broke, struggling, exactly the same. She had left, and they had forgotten about her. She asked once about having a friend over, and Julia made a face. "We value our privacy," she said, and that was that.

Vivian had been cut off, almost entirely, from her old life. Jonathan and Julia had become everything to her. She loved them, and she knew that she should not love them. She had heard Julia explain the relationship to Jonathan. "She gets a paycheck," Julia said. "We can't let ourselves get confused."

It was crazy how much that hurt Vivian's feelings. Even though Julia herself had admitted to being confused.

It felt strange to Vivian to have a growing bank account. She also liked it. She deserved it. Parts of her job were so strange, like keeping Jonathan's wardrobe up to date. He was extremely particular. He wanted a certain number of socks, white T-shirts, button-down shirts, cashmere sweaters. If he got new socks, he wanted the old socks thrown out. He got angry if he had too many pairs of socks. It was upsetting when Jonathan got angry at her. She had cried once when she'd ordered the wrong food for dinner, and he had hugged her, called her Vivvy, and she had let him comfort her. She'd sunk into the hug, felt his shirt grow wet with her tears.

That, she said to herself, was fucked up.

Vivian fed Julia's feral cats, and when she spent time with Julia, she petted and played with the domesticated ones. While Vivian did not love these cats, she knew that it was important to act as if she did. Vivian was not clear on her responsibilities when it came to Julia. Jonathan often reminded Vivian that she worked for him, but Julia was always giving her things to do.

She ate meals with the Fosters.

She played Scrabble with them when it rained, an activity that she hated. Julia could not spell and Jonathan got annoyed when Vivian won, but she could not get herself to lose on purpose.

They seemed to compete for her affection, to see who could make her laugh more, pay her the biggest compliment. Once, after she had been living in their guesthouse for a few months, Julia asked Vivian if she was interested in anything more. Vivian shook her head. Right away. Even though she did not ask Julia what she meant, even though she wanted to say yes. What *had* she meant?

Vivian had stopped talking to her adoptive parents, and Julia knew this. It had come out once in conversation. Maybe Julia was offering her career advice. An opportunity for advancement.

But that wasn't it.

The "more."

A threesome. That was too twisted. That could not have been what Julia meant. Vivian hated herself for even thinking that. Jonathan and Julia were more like her parents. Maybe they could adopt her and then she would not have to feel ashamed about the paycheck. But that would mean that they would stop paying her. Besides, they could not adopt her. She already had adoptive parents. Wouldn't it be funny if Jonathan was somehow her actual dad? But he had never been to Vietnam. She had asked him.

All the time, she found them looking at her.

Like *looking* at her. As if she was naked. She felt naked.

Jonathan used to tell Vivian that she was beautiful, and then Julia told him that he had to stop. "Though you are beautiful," Julia said, laughing.

They all laughed.

Vivian never told them she wanted to be a writer. She was afraid they would laugh at her. Their little Vivian wanted to be a writer. She was afraid that they would laugh at her and then encourage her. She could not bear it. She would not tell them.

It was her secret. Precious. Shameful. She did not know why.

⟋

In the beginning, Vivian really thought she had the best job ever. Amazing bosses. Free rent, safety from the pandemic. Free groceries. The Fosters were the smartest, most interesting, most glamorous people she had ever met, and they cared about her.

Everything started to change when Julia had her research Vietnamese orphanages. Vivian got this feeling, a tightness in her chest. Julia started asking Vivian questions about her white Midwestern adoptive parents. She wanted to know if Vivian felt assimilated. She actually wanted to know if Vivian had watched *Modern Family* and what Vivian thought of Lily. Vivian was surprised that Julia had watched *Modern Family*. But Lily had come up in Google searches; that's how she knew about her. Julia never watched popular TV. Suddenly, they were all watching *Modern Family* together.

Like it was research.

Vivian had become research for them.

This felt like part of the unspoken "more." Like too much.

"I don't want to talk about my parents," Vivian told her. Vivian was afraid that Julia would be angry with her.

"Julia," Jonathan said, turning off the episode of *Modern*

Family where Lily's dads took her to a Vietnamese restaurant and Lily hated the food. "You can't compare Vivian to a character on a TV show."

"Agreed," Julia said. "But I can take an interest."

Vivian, of course, had been compared to Lily for years. She had envied Lily her gay parents. Vivian's parents were conservative. They went to church each week, Vivian wearing a dress and shiny shoes. There were family albums with photos of her mother beaming at a baby Vivian. Vivian was five when her mother got pregnant, something the doctors had said was impossible, and had a boy. A boy. Vivian's role in the family changed. She became more like the nanny, the live-in maid. Vivian identified with Harry Potter, whose aunt and uncle kept him in the cupboard under the stairs, more than she did with the much-loved Lily from *Modern Family*. Except no one ever came to rescue her. No Hagrid. No owls. She just had to grow up. Vivian had been trained basically almost from birth to be a personal assistant, which might be why she was so good at her job.

Julia solved Jonathan's challenge, of course. The hot air balloon in the swimming pool. It was just a phone call. Usually, that was all it was. She told them to charge Jonathan's card for the damage to the hot air balloon, the retrieval from the swimming pool. It was amazing how easy it was to solve problems when you did not have to worry about how much it cost.

It would have been Vivian's fault if they had died.

Vivian could not get that thought out of her head.

She had watched Julia get dressed. "Jonathan likes the blue dress," Vivian told her.

"I don't care what Jonathan likes," Julia said.

But she wore the blue dress.

Vivian had driven them to the launch.

"Have fun!" she'd called out. "Good luck."

They blew her kisses.

She watched the hot air balloon rise.

Part of her was hurt that they had not asked her to go with them.

It looked fun. Exciting.

They had not died. They had not gotten hurt.

Vivian took the ten thousand dollars from Jonathan's desk, all of it, and put it in her pocket. She knew that there were security cameras in the house. She did not care. What were they going to do? Ask for it back? Call the police? She *knew* things about them.

Anyway, Jonathan seemed to have forgotten about the money. It was such a small amount. To him. That was why its very existence was so insulting. It was not a small amount to her.

Vivian did not know why she felt the way she felt.

Full of rage.

She did not like it.

Joannie

Joannie was surprised to be enjoying herself as much as she was. She liked waking up in someone else's home. It was so *clean*. The bedsheets had been so nice, crisp. The bottom sheet had not come off the corners of the mattress. It was a wonderful, spacious bed, and Lucy had rolled all the way to the other side, instead of crowding her out the way she usually did. Joannie had slept well.

Now she was in a kitchen that could be in a Nancy Meyers movie. She opened the refrigerator to look for half-and-half for her coffee and found fresh raspberries, strawberries, and blueberries. Butter in a butter dish. There was half-and-half. The inside of this refrigerator could be photographed for a magazine. And Johnny did, in fact, make Lucy bacon, though he had momentarily joked about not having any. Joannie did not love the fact that he had teased her daughter. Men, in general, tended to tease girls. Women, too. Joannie did not understand or appreciate it. No one ever enjoyed being teased. He did let Lucy eat an entire pint of raspberries without saying a word.

Joannie genuinely enjoyed her breakfast. All of it. She had heard Julia the night before, the gasps and moans on the other side of the wall, and she had been surprised. Her foremost desire, when kissing Johnny, after all, had been to make it stop. She had possibly brought the hot air balloon down from the sky with the power of her mind.

Joannie wondered who had *not* heard Julia: Jonathan, Lucy, the boy in the basement. But it was fine. Joannie did not want Johnny. She was more than happy to sleep with her daughter. Joannie did not actually know if she was even capable of having sex again. With another person, at least. It had been so long.

She was not, however, completely unsocialized. She did not, for instance, mind the company of others. She was able to make conversation with Julia and Johnny. She was up to date on current events and new shows on Netflix, and held an opinion on most subjects. Julia had asked Joannie for a sheet of paper from her sketch pad, and now Julia was making a drawing of her daughter. This was unexpected in so many ways.

Joannie did not think Lucy could sit still, but she was wrong, and the drawing itself was beautiful. Julia, it turned out, was a real artist. Joannie happily drank her coffee and ate her bacon and one large fluffy pancake and watched, mesmerized, as Lucy's face appeared on the piece of paper. It was as good as Joannie had felt in a long while.

"You are so talented," she said.

Julia was the kind of artist who could draw a portrait that was like a photograph. It was amazing, and Joannie was amazed.

Julia tucked a strand of hair behind her ear.

"I went to art school," she said.

"Oh," Joannie said, surprised.

"Most people don't know shit about me," Julia said. "Except for the fact that I am married to Jonathan Foster."

"I suppose that could be considered a coup," Joannie said, taken aback by Julia's bitterness. Joannie was of the belief that rich people really had no right to be as unhappy as they often appeared to be. If Joannie were rich, she would be significantly more happy. She was sure of this.

"True," Julia said.

"Can I have that?" Joannie asked. "The drawing. When you are done."

Maybe, she thought, she was not properly socialized after all. Joannie could see Julia hesitate, look up from her piece of paper and back at Lucy and back down at her paper.

"I sell my work," she said. "For a lot of money."

"Oh," Joannie said, realizing that she was not supposed to have asked. "I'm sorry. I wasn't thinking. How much would you want for it?"

Julia shook her head. "No, of course, of course you can have it. It's your daughter. It's coming out nicely. I always hate giving up my work. Selling paintings. I have trouble letting them go."

"Mommy will give you a flower painting," Lucy said.

"That's okay," Julia said.

Clearly, Julia did not want Joannie's amateur flowers, but Joannie wished she could have lied. To spare her feelings. Some people were like that.

"I want to draw," Tyson said.

Neither Joannie nor Julia responded.

"One second, Ty," Johnny said.

Joannie did not like this nickname for the boy. It would make sense, really, for her to offer Johnny a hand—he was busy at the stove—and yet she didn't. She didn't want to help. He had told her to relax. Somehow, the entire vibe in the room had changed. It was Julia's fault. If only she could have said yes to a flower painting. Joannie could hear the voice of her ex-husband. *You never let yourself be happy, Joannie.* It was something he always used to say. That voice. It was so damning, so critical, and after having been divorced for so many years already, she wanted that voice out of her head.

Joannie stood up, and then realized that she had to go somewhere, get out of that kitchen. She no longer wanted to sit at a table with Julia. "I am going to go check on Jonathan," she said, even though she had absolutely no interest in checking on Jonathan.

It was possible that she had hurt the man's feelings the night before. She was also relieved that she had not let him touch her. It wasn't payback. She just had not wanted to.

Now, in the bright light of the day, Jonathan beamed at her. "So it's you," he said.

Joannie could not hide her confusion. Had he been expecting her?

"I was wondering who would come outside first," he said.

Joannie nodded, though this statement did not make sense to her.

"My assistant, Vivian, is taking care of the hot air balloon."

Joannie nodded again. Of course, it would not make sense to leave a hot air balloon at the bottom of a stranger's swimming pool. He had a woman, Vivian, fixing his mistake. Joannie walked over to the pool to look at the hot air balloon. That was such a crazy thing, the way it had fallen out of the sky.

Joannie had not wanted to talk to Julia, and she did not particularly want to talk to Jonathan either. It was crazy that she was still there. It was the next day. After breakfast, Joannie and Lucy were going to have to leave, and Joannie was not looking forward to that. Lucy would want to know what they were going to do. Did they have plans? They never had plans. Not before the pandemic, definitely not during the pandemic, and not now, when life was starting to get back to normal. In and of itself, the date with Johnny was a very big deal. Now Joannie wanted to stay in this house. She wanted to be fed lunch and then dinner and swim laps in the pool and watch TV on the enormous television set in the comfortable basement. She did not ever want to go home, really.

"You saved my life," Jonathan said.

He joined her at the pool. He seemed intent on talking to her. Joannie should have stayed in the kitchen. Julia had really not said or done anything terrible. Maybe she had not even heard Lucy offer her a painting. This conversation now, with Jonathan, was her own fault.

"You would have been fine," Joannie said.

"There is no way to know for sure," Jonathan said. "I only know what happened."

"That's true."

Joannie sat down at the edge of the pool and put her feet in the water. There was an episode of *The Simpsons* where a family came to visit and never left. She could lock Johnny out, somehow, but she was not sure what to do about Tyson. Surely he could go live with his mother across the street.

"You'll be wanting a reward," Jonathan said.

"A reward? No, of course not," Joannie responded right away, and then she wished she hadn't. Jonathan Foster was the CEO of a tech company that was practically infamous. Chances were good he would have risen to the surface of the pool and pulled himself out, but she was the one who had gone in. Not Johnny. Not Julia. She had saved his life.

"Well, I'll think on it," Jonathan said. "Something appropriate. Maybe summer camp for Lucy."

Joannie sighed.

Summer camp. A small blip.

She had blown it, the way she often did. Joannie wanted a real reward. For saving Jonathan Foster's life. A million dollars. "I think saving your life is worth more than that," she said. She had wanted to sound flippant but was pretty sure she had failed.

"We'll work it out," Jonathan said. "I'll ask Vivian what she thinks."

"You seem to ask your assistant for a lot of things," Joannie said.

Jonathan nodded. "I would be lost without her."

"Can I see her picture?" Joannie asked.

"You want to see a picture of my assistant?" Jonathan asked.

Joannie shrugged. It was a strange thing to ask. "You talk about her with affection," Joannie said. "I'm curious."

"Everybody should have an assistant," Jonathan said.

Jonathan sat down next to Joannie at the pool.

He put his feet in the water. Joannie looked down at her feet. His feet. Jonathan scrolled through his phone and showed her a picture of himself with a beautiful young Asian woman in a short black dress with long shining hair and clunky black glasses. She barely came up to his shoulder. She looked young enough to be his daughter. Jonathan was beaming at the picture of her.

"She's not your secret daughter?" Joannie asked.

Jonathan blushed.

"Girlfriend?"

Jonathan shook his head.

"I like her too much," Jonathan said. "You can tell?"

Joannie took a deep breath, said nothing.

"No," he said. "We're not involved. Obviously. I am considerably older. I am also her employer. I behave appropriately. Always."

"She's a baby," Joannie said.

"She's twenty-four," Jonathan said.

"That's baby territory," Joannie said. "Think about what you were like when you were twenty-four."

"God," Jonathan said.

"It's one thing to cheat on your wife, but it's another to do it with a child."

"She's not a child," Jonathan said.

"Not from a technical standpoint."

"And I am not," Jonathan said. "I wouldn't."

"Good," Joannie said. "Because I hear she is an excellent assistant. You wouldn't want to jeopardize that."

Jonathan smiled. His whole body, Joannie realized, relaxed. She could not believe that she had spoken to him so plainly. He had been an asshole when he was a teenager. There was no reason to believe that he had changed.

"Did you hear that show last night?" Jonathan asked.

Now Joannie really wished she was back in the kitchen. Or that she could go into the pool, put her head underwater. This was a conversation she did not want to engage in.

"Maybe that's all it was," Joannie said. It was always her impulse. To be kind. "What you heard. A great big show."

"Real." Jonathan smirked. "I know those sounds."

"Bully for you," Joannie said.

She remembered. Sex, what a big deal it was, in a marriage. Her ex always knew how long it had been since the last time, and he remembered, too, what kind of sex it was, because blow jobs somehow counted for less than actual intercourse. At one point, they were having sex every day, not because she wanted to, but because he had insisted that not only would it improve the marriage, but that Joannie would be much happier, too. And she supposed that she *was* happier, because her ex-husband was so much nicer to be around in this period of constant intercourse. He had been right, but then a day came when Joannie just couldn't do it anymore. Followed by the next day and the day after. She couldn't do it. The nice phase came to a notable end.

"You know," Jonathan said, "if Lucy hadn't come crashing into our room—"

Julia shook her head, and thankfully, Jonathan stopped talking. It was so boring. Sex. It was so annoying even to have to think about it, right then, on a beautiful day, looking out at the swimming pool. People seemed to care so goddamned much about sex. Jonathan had basically admitted to lusting after his twenty-four-year-old assistant. If the topic ever came up again, Joannie would take his reward money, but she didn't believe that the offer was real. She could bring it back up, but how could she slide it into conversation? Joannie could use the money. She had published a novel, but that was years ago; the advance was spent, the royalty checks smaller each time. The child support she received was minimal, her free-lance work had dried up during the pandemic, and the adjunct teaching was not worth her time. Really, she had to get a job or she would not be able to afford the apartment she didn't want to live in anymore. How long would it be until she and Lucy were homeless? Joannie's thoughts were starting to spi-ral. This happened sometimes. She had woken up happy.

"Your wife, Julia, is a talented artist," Joannie said.

"She can draw anything," Jonathan said.

"She is sketching Lucy right now," Joannie said.

Inside, Joannie heard laughter. Lucy was howling with laughter. Joannie could see that Julia had her arm affection-ately around her daughter, and this seemed strange. They had only met this morning. Joannie was jealous. Not because Julia had slept with Johnny, but because she had made Lucy laugh.

"Watch out," Jonathan said. "Because my wife wants a little girl."

Joannie thought about the pretty assistant's picture on the phone. "So do you," she said.

"Ouch," Jonathan said. "It is not the same. And please do not presume to think you know me."

"I wouldn't dare," Joannie said.

And while she did not think it had been Jonathan's intention to make her cry, his words had come out harsh, like a slap in the face, and she suddenly very much did want to cry. In fact, she *was* crying, which was embarrassing, and she did not know how to make it stop.

Joannie thought she would just slide into the pool, swim away from him, but she was wearing sweatpants, and that would be so awkward, he would know that she had gotten into the pool just to get away from him, and that was stupid and childlike, and then she would have to ask Johnny for more clothes, or more likely, she would have to go home to get something to change into because the man could not have unlimited clean sweatpants, and once she went home, that would be it, they would never be invited back, and then the tears started to stream down Joannie's face, unchecked.

Jonathan, clearly, was the kind of man who could not bear to see a woman cry. And because he needed to make the tears stop, he leaned forward and put one hand on the back of her head and the other on the small of her back, which felt so *good,* and he kissed her. And this kiss was different. It was not Johnny from last night, smothering her. It was like that first kiss, when Joannie was fourteen years old and making out with this beautiful boy she had just met.

And while Joannie did not like the adult Jonathan Foster or even think she was attracted to him, he was an incredible kisser, and it had been so long since Joannie had been kissed so well. He kissed the tears off her face and kissed her neck and then her lips, and when he broke away, Joannie said, "Again," as if she were Lucy wanting more, and Jonathan grinned, and he kissed her again, and then Joannie could hear Lucy screaming at her, screaming, "Mommy, stop! Mommy, stop kissing that man!"

And still, Joannie didn't stop kissing that man because he was kissing her, and Lucy ran outside and came barreling straight at Joannie, and probably because Joannie had been busy kissing and not thinking about Lucy's safety, somehow they all ended up in the swimming pool, Jonathan and Joannie and Lucy, and Joannie started to laugh. Of course, she could not, should not, kiss Jonathan Foster. Maybe it was not, consciously, Lucy's intention, but Joannie wasn't allowed anything for herself.

Johnny

Johnny was pretty sure that nothing had happened between Joannie and Jonathan the night before, but there they were, making out at the swimming pool like teenagers. He wasn't pleased. Julia watched him watching them, an amused smile on her face, and then Lucy saw what they saw.

"No!" Lucy cried.

She went running out the back door and straight toward the pool, and didn't stop. She crashed right into Joannie and Jonathan and all three of them went into the water.

"Not again," Johnny said, slapping his forehead with his hand.

"Not again," Tyson repeated, slapping his forehead with his hand.

Johnny thought about his homeowner's insurance. He might be liable if his guests drowned. He was not even sure if there was adequate chlorine in the water or, alternatively, much too much. One had to be careful having guests over. They could always sue. Or, they could have sex with the wrong person. Johnny did not think that was what he had done, but maybe that was what he had done. Maybe he wanted to have sex with the woman in the swimming pool, laughing.

He was hungover.

This was happening too often.

He blamed it on the pandemic.

There was nothing to do every night but sit in front of the TV and drink. Smoke weed.

He thought he should go in after them, but this was not a downed-hot-air-balloon situation. His guests were able to get out of the pool on their own. No one was drowning. He would have to provide more dry clothes. Maybe, he thought, it was time for everyone to go home. Maybe he was done hosting.

Then the back gate opened and in came his ex-wife, Fern, with their dog, Coco, wagging her tail, barking like a lunatic. They shared custody of not only the boy but also the dog. Really, Coco was Fern's dog, but Johnny kept her when Fern went out of town. He loved the dog. He loved Fern. He loved his family. It had not been his idea to get divorced. There were just too many things that Fern did not love about him. The list had been shockingly long, ending with his gender and a false accusation of rape. Sex she had had with him when she had not particularly wanted to. Fern had decided she was not attracted to men. Johnny wished she had come to this understanding before she married him.

Now she lived across the street and was always around. Fern knew about his date with Joannie and probably wanted to hear all the details. Still, she should have waited. She had no right to let herself in. He had told her to use the front door. Ring the bell. But that wasn't like Fern. Also, she was there to pick up Tyson. She always claimed to forget not to let herself in. Anyway, there she was, and she was sure to have opinions. Fern always had opinions.

Johnny watched as she took it all in: Joannie and Lucy and Jonathan in the pool. The hot air balloon at the bottom of the pool. Tyson came running outside, looking as if he was going to jump in, too, but Fern grabbed him. "I don't think so, mister."

Johnny waved at his ex-wife.

Put on a happy face.

That was what he did. It usually worked. Look at his glorious life. Look at all the people in the swimming pool. This could be a scene in a movie.

"Everything all right here?" Fern called.

Joannie and Lucy swam together to the shallow end of the pool and came out, climbing the steps. Jonathan pulled himself out of the deep end.

"What were you thinking?" Joannie asked Lucy. "You could have hurt someone."

"Mommy." Lucy hugged her mom. "Mommy. Mom. My mommy."

Joannie kissed the top of her daughter's head and held her close. Johnny would have screamed at Tyson if he had acted so recklessly.

"Anybody hurt?" Johnny asked.

Jonathan shook water out of his ear.

"Just wet," he said sheepishly.

Julia emerged from the kitchen. Johnny wondered what had taken her so long. He felt his face turn red. He was like a boy.

"This looks like quite a party," Fern said.

Johnny grinned. Fern had recently broken up with her girlfriend, said that it was getting too serious, and now she was around even more. If that was possible. Johnny realized that he was going to have to set some boundaries. He looked at his wet guests, at his ex-wife. His gaze settled on Julia, who was beautiful, really. There was no hope there, was there?

"Who needs more coffee?" he asked. "Dry clothes?"

Jonathan laughed and raised his hand.

"I'll take some coffee," Fern said. "And an explanation."

This hit Johnny the wrong way. Maybe it was the hangover. Or the fact that she thought she was so goddamned superior to him, deserved an explanation.

"I don't owe you explanations anymore," Johnny said.

"Oh, hush," Fern said. "You have a hot air balloon in your swimming pool. Can't a girl be curious?"

"We had a sleepover party," Tyson called out. "This is my friend Lucy."

"Hi, Lucy," Fern said.

Lucy and Joannie had gotten out of the pool, were dripping wet.

"I'll get more clothes," Johnny said.

"More clothes?" Fern asked.

"Lucy can wear my clothes!" Tyson screamed.

"I'll make more coffee," Julia said.

Johnny was surprised.

"My clothes from last night should be dry," Joannie offered. Johnny had not had a chance to talk to her privately. Things had been going well, their date, up until the hot air balloon. Maybe it was not too late. Maybe this was a story that they could laugh about years from now. He wanted both of them. Julia and Joannie. He was done with Fern.

"I'll find you something," Johnny said. "Don't worry."

Fern could think what she liked. It would be funny to watch her try to figure it all out. Johnny wondered if last night was one of the best he'd ever had. No one had drowned. There would be no lawsuit. His son was happy. He had made a woman, a beautiful woman, a stranger, come. Coco wagged her tail. She had stopped barking. His ex-wife frowned. The sun shined upon them all.

Julia

Falling in love with someone else's child was not the way to go. Julia watched as the little girl ran outside to get her mother away from Jonathan. It was comical when they all fell in the pool, but then Julia realized that it could have been dangerous. One of them could have hit their head, drowned.

Julia had never had maternal instincts. Which made it especially stupid, that late last gasp of wanting a baby. For wanting, even, a life with Jonathan, who had been an avowed bachelor playboy until he married her.

It had been one more moment of folly, drawing this girl, imagining some kind of future with her. She had snapped at the girl's mother, too. She'd heard it in her voice, how pissed off she was. She didn't want to give away her drawing. It was a great drawing. But she had made a fool of herself. Ungenerous, as always. Which was ironic since all she did was give away money.

She really had to get the fuck out of this house. Before she made one more mistake. She couldn't take back what had happened with Johnny. He had turned beet red when he saw her. She could have him again, but what would be the point of that? She had entered her marriage in good faith—and then she had ended it. It was satisfying to be that effective. But maybe she could take it back. She had not thought it through. What her life would look like. After.

If she lost Jonathan.

She would still be rich.

She would be fine.

But when she didn't hate Jonathan, she appreciated her life with him. They took wonderful vacations. They ate wonderful meals together. They used to have good sex. Last night could have been good for Jonathan. Probably, he had never considered the possibility that she would also cheat.

She wandered over to her wet husband. He had been kissing Joannie. He put his arm around Julia.

"Morning, sweetheart," he said.

It was such a relief. They would act as if nothing had happened. "Look at you," she said. "Back in the pool. Honestly, I'm ready to go home. What about you?"

"Home sounds good," Jonathan said.

Julia had no idea what he was thinking. It was maddening, really, what a good actor he was.

"I'm sorry," Julia said, kissing his hand. She *was* sorry. She had not needed to make such a public show. Really, she hadn't been thinking. She was going to stop drinking again.

She watched as Lucy and her mom went into the house. She knew, because Lucy had told her in the ten minutes that they had talked, that they lived in an apartment around the corner, above a bakery, something Lucy found embarrassing, because she sometimes ran into kids from school having breakfast, kids who didn't even know what apartments were because everyone else lived in a big house. Everyone. Lucy had told her that she wanted to live in a big house like the one Tyson lived in. Poor kid, Julia had thought, and then she had thought about real poor kids. As a wealthy person, she found it more comfortable talking to other wealthy people.

She could help Lucy.

She loved how Lucy just talked to her, told her everything. She was sure that Joannie would be appalled to have had her life laid out like that. Listening to Lucy, Julia wondered if she had crossed a line. Not only in her marriage but with this single mother and her little girl. Maybe Lucy had thought her mom was going to marry Johnny and that the boy was going to be her brother. The big house was going to be hers. Maybe Joannie had wanted that, too. Julia's mother had once told Julia that she was an agent of chaos. It was one of the cruelest things anyone had ever said to her.

She leaned into Jonathan's shoulder.

This situation was a mess. They needed to leave.

"I texted Vivian," he said. "Someone is coming over to get the balloon."

"Thank God for Vivian," Julia said. "Can you ask her to get us a car?"

"Absolutely," he said.

He kissed the top of Julia's head.

Julia wondered if Jonathan could have actual feelings for Joannie. They had, after all, been kissing. Maybe that could somehow work, Jonathan pairing with Joannie. She could take the girl instead of Johnny. Because they could be good for the girl. She could not outright buy the girl a house. But maybe she could set up a college fund, private school. Clearly, she wasn't over the girl. So even though she had just told Jonathan to call them a car, maybe it was too soon to leave.

She had to tell herself to slow down. Her recent ADHD diagnosis had been a relief. It explained so much. How easily distracted she was. Always in a rush. Starting new projects before she finished old ones. The mania in her brain. She took the pills that were prescribed to her and felt focused. She felt on fire and calm, all at the same time. It occurred to her that she had not taken her pill that morning, but she had some in her bag.

She squeezed Jonathan's hand. To make sure that the connection was still there, real. It was rage, she realized, that she had felt the night before, but now it was gone.

There was a new person at the pool, a woman with short hair, holding a barking Labrador retriever on a leash.

"I'm Fern," this new woman said.

"Fern," Julia repeated. She had not asked, had no interest in her. "I'm Julia," Julia said.

Fern stared at her.

Fuck. She was making Julia work.

"How do you know Johnny?" Julia asked.

"How do I know my ex-husband?" Fern said. "Father of my child."

Julia shrugged. How was she supposed to have known? Jonathan laughed. He was not helping her.

"How do *you* know Johnny?" Fern asked.

Julia pointed to the hot air balloon in the bottom of the pool.

"Crash landing," she said.

If Joannie or Jonathan was not upset with her, this angry lesbian ex-wife seemed to be. Sure, Johnny was a mistake. She had just been so angry at Jonathan. She supposed she had gotten back at him. She remembered, again, the scene from the kitchen window, watching Jonathan and Joannie kiss; there was a surprising amount of tenderness to it. Julia was jealous. She had wanted to break something. Throw her plate full of food. Thank goodness Lucy had put an end to it.

Jonathan shook Fern's hand.

He could be charming in the most absurd situations. This was one of them.

"Jonathan Foster," he said.

"*The* Jonathan Foster," Fern said.

He loved when people recognized him, knew his name. It was pathetic how much pleasure that gave him.

"Well, it depends," he said. "But pretty sure that's me."

"I'm here to pick up Tyson," Fern said. "But this looks like too much fun."

"Mommy," Tyson said, hugging her, petting the dog. "We had the best time. Daddy let us stay up as late as we wanted."

This kid, of course, was the child of Johnny and Fern. She

clearly had not always been a lesbian. All of these people, in these suburban towns, had children. It was unfair that she could not have one.

"When will the car get here?" she asked Jonathan. Her first instinct had been right. They needed to leave.

"I'll text Vivian," he said.

"I can get an Uber if that's easier," Julia said. "You can stay if you want."

Jonathan shook his head. He had issues with privacy, calling cars, which was his reason for relying on Vivian.

"Don't be ridiculous," he said. "We arrived together, and we are leaving together."

"Don't leave," Johnny called out. "It's almost time for lunch."

That was ridiculous. It was still morning. The breakfast was still on the table.

"We have to go," Julia said.

"Why?" Jonathan asked. "Why do we have to go?"

"Because I want to," Julia said.

"We don't have any plans," Jonathan said. "Our calendar is clear."

"Our calendars are never clear," Julia said. "Ever."

"It's our anniversary weekend," Jonathan said. "Vivian thought it was a good idea. I had more planned for us. Actually, I had nothing planned. Just time. To spend with you."

Julia was going to pretend to gag. She was going to say something catty about their anniversary, then about Vivian, about Vivian being the third person in their marriage, in their life, but she genuinely liked Vivian. She was the one who had encouraged Jonathan to give her more and more responsibility. Who had suggested that Vivian move into the guesthouse when the pandemic hit.

"I am tired," Julia said.

"I am, too," Jonathan said. "I can't tell you the last time I had to sleep on a couch."

Julia stayed quiet.

"Killer on my back," he said. "But you started this."

"I started nothing," Julia said. "Last night was nothing."

"Best nothing I ever had," Johnny said.

Both Julia and Jonathan stared at him. He was a complete idiot. It would have been just as easy to keep his mouth shut. What, did he want credit? She almost hoped that Jonathan would punch him. But it was better not to react, and Jonathan did not react.

"What nothing happened last night?" Fern asked, petting Coco.

"We watched two Harry Potter movies," Tyson said. "Two."

"You don't have to worry about the hot air balloon," Jonathan told her.

"I'm not worried," Fern said. "This is not my house anymore."

"Then why are you here?" Jonathan asked.

"Well," Fern said. She looked annoyed, but that was fine. "We have plans for the day. I had to make sure Tyson was ready."

"We do?" Tyson asked. "Can Lucy come?"

"Who is Lucy?" Fern asked.

"My friend Lucy," Tyson said. "Who slept over. She's still here! She is getting dressed. She just fell into the pool."

"I can ask her mother," Fern said. "Where is her mother?"

"She's getting dressed," Johnny said.

It was so interesting to Julia, how jealous this woman was, a divorced lesbian, coming over, acting like it was her house. Julia was almost tempted to tell her about Johnny. Julia could be perverse that way. Sometimes she enjoyed hurting other people for no reason at all. It was something she actually liked about herself. Johnny had practically announced that they'd had sex, like he was proud of himself. Probably he wanted his ex-wife to know. Julia supported him on that.

Jonathan shook his head.

"Deep breath," he said to Julia.

She had gotten into trouble before, in the press, speaking her mind, not thinking first. Jonathan could be condescending, but he was right. Julia just needed to take her pill. It was one of her favorite moments of the day. Taking her pill.

"Is Tyson ready for soccer?" Fern asked Johnny.

"Oops," Johnny said. "I forgot."

"Of course you forgot."

Fern and Tyson went into the house with the dog, and Johnny followed. It was a relief, having him gone. Julia's pill was also inside the house, in her bag, but she could wait another minute.

"I think I pissed her off," Julia said.

"Why did you do that?" Jonathan said.

Julia was at a loss for words.

"You don't want to leave?" she asked Jonathan.

"I have to admit that I am amused by this situation."

"You're amused."

"You're not?" Jonathan asked. "It's interesting, you have to admit."

"Jonathan," Julia said.

"I'm not upset," he said. "I mean, I was at first."

"And now you're not," Julia said. That was fast. "What changed?"

"Joannie," he said.

Joannie.

She had not expected him to say that.

"You want to get involved with a single mother?" she said. "I thought you were smarter than that."

"I don't want to get involved," he said. "I might just like to help her. I actually do feel bad. About how I treated her all those years ago. I might have also mentioned a reward. For saving my life."

"Her daughter is smart," Julia said. "And she's lovely. Really lovely."

"You see?" Jonathan said.

"They are people," Julia said. "Not pets."

"I know that."

"Do you?"

They had done this before, adopted people. Vivian, for instance. She had been a temp. Hired to cover a receptionist's maternity leave. And now she was Jonathan's personal assistant. She lived in the guesthouse on their property. She was family. They both doted on her.

"This will be different," Jonathan said.

"Why will it be different?" Julia said.

"Because I want it to be," Jonathan said.

"I want the little girl," Julia said.

It was true.

"I'll take the mother."

Julia was not sure about this.

"What about Johnny?" Jonathan said.

"What about him?" Julia said. "You can't just have the mother. She is a person." She was aware of the fact that she might have just contradicted herself. "And besides that, I don't want him."

"You could have fooled me," Jonathan said.

"Exactly," Julia said. "That's what I did."

"Let's just stay through lunch."

"Lunch," Julia said. "Jesus."

Jonathan took off his wet T-shirt and then his sweatpants. He was wearing underwear, fortunately.

"What are you doing?" Julia asked.

"My clothes are wet."

She had not seen him undressed in many months.

But she had just seen him kissing the mother, leaning in, touching her hair, and now she felt some sort of desire for him. It was exciting, to want Jonathan again. She reached out for his penis, visible through his wet boxer shorts, and it immediately responded. Julia was glad. She did not want to blow up her life.

"You look good," Julia said.

"A compliment," Jonathan said.

"A compliment," Julia said.

Jonathan kissed her.

His skin was wet. He tasted like Jonathan.

"Was he good?" Jonathan whispered. "Last night?"

"I am not going to answer that," Julia said.

"I heard you," Jonathan said. "I heard you."

"So you have your answer," Julia said.

Jonathan grinned. He was actually beaming. The sun was shining on him, like he was some kind of fucking Adonis. Perfect in his boxer shorts. Of course, he was perfect. He worked out with a trainer. Played tennis. They had a chef making them well-balanced, delicious meals. She wasn't going to blow up their life. It was a good life.

"Life's good, Julia," Jonathan said, reading her mind. "Be happy. Look at this beautiful day. I have been so bored lately. Haven't you? And stressed. The baby business. It has felt awfully sad, hasn't it? And look at us now. Stocks are up. The sun is shining. We survived the Great Hot Air Balloon Crash of 2021."

"Is that what we are going to call it?" Julia said.

"That's what I am going to call it. Let's let this man cook us lunch."

"So you are jealous?" Julia said. "At least a little bit?"

As soon as she said it, Julia wished she could take it back. He was not supposed to know that she cared. She had not thought that she cared. She didn't care. But clearly, she cared.

"Of course I am jealous," Jonathan said. "Why do you think I didn't sleep?"

"The couch was uncomfortable," Julia said.

"That too."

"You were jealous?" Julia asked again.

Here was something she hadn't told him.

The hot air balloon had been magic. Flying over the fields of grass, the houses, the coast. She had loved it—the view, the air, the roar of the flames keeping them up high. She had loved it all until the winds picked up and she realized that he did not know what the fuck he was doing and they were going to die. She had been almost pleased with that moment of clarity, too. The great Jonathan Foster did not have a fucking clue. Which would have been okay, except they could have died. But for a few minutes, before they landed in Johnny's backyard, she had thought they might. And when Jonathan fell out of the balloon basket headfirst into the pool, for a moment, she had thought she might inherit all his money. And she had been glad.

Joannie

After lunch, Joannie decided to run home to pick up a few things. Her apartment had never looked smaller, messier. Her apartment made her feel like her entire life was a mistake. She even wondered about returning to Johnny's house. It was not a good thing, jumping into other people's lives, because eventually she was going to have to go home, and stay home.

Lucy had wanted to come with her, but Julia had convinced her to stay. Joannie was grateful the girl had listened. It gave Joannie a chance to breathe. She knew that she should rush, return as quickly as possible, and she wanted to do that, she wanted to get the hell out of her apartment and go back to a nice world that was not hers, but instead she sat on the couch.

Joannie wanted to get a new couch. The leather on one of the cushions was cracked and broken, and Julia had covered the gash with duct tape. It was fancy duct tape, duct tape that had a whale pattern, but still, it was duct tape.

For reasons she did not understand, Jonathan Foster was trying to woo her. Their kiss by the pool had been interrupted by Lucy, but during lunch, he had held her hand, caressed it under the table. The caress, as much as the kiss, had given her actual tingles, and while Joannie wanted to be categorically against Jonathan, she wasn't.

She had thought she might be attracted to Julia, but those feelings had shifted, and now she wanted to kiss Jonathan again. She remembered seeing him for the first time when she was fourteen, realizing right away that he was out of her league, and still, somehow, they had ended up walking around the grounds, and finally kissing, making out, standing up behind the stables. The kiss at the pool had felt dangerous, because of what had happened before, the hurt of that rejection, but she was a different person now. He could not hurt her, because she did not care. Which was a load of shit. Of course she cared.

She already felt preemptively hurt.

She was in love with Johnny's house. But Julia had proposed that after lunch they go to the Fosters' house. "Lucy wants to see the cats," she said.

"Mommy wants to see your swimming pool," Lucy said.

It was a big mistake, Joannie had a feeling, but it was the plan. When in doubt, her ex-husband used to say, stick to the plan. Maybe this was the only useful thing he'd ever said to her. Lucy was having the best time, and this made Joannie happy. First a sleepover. Then bacon. Soon a waterslide on the back of Jonathan Foster's motorboat. He had shown Lucy a picture of the boat. He had shown Joannie a picture of his assistant.

Joannie had done so many things for her daughter. She had made sacrifices. She did not know what else to do. She wondered if she could do something to make them both happy. It seemed impossible. Joannie was not used to considering her own happiness. She had navigated her way out of a life of misery, and for the longest time that had seemed like enough. It was stupid to want more. She did love the plants in her apartment. She told herself that.

She had only been gone a day.

⟶

Johnny would not be coming with them.

It appeared that he very much wanted to come, but Fern had returned, insisting that he come to his son's soccer game. It was an actual game that afternoon, not a practice.

Joannie was going to go to the Fosters' estate and take Lucy out on a boat. And swim in their pool. Jonathan had told her that she would like his pool, as if it was a contest, and Joannie was fairly certain that Jonathan would win.

"There is a hot tub, too," Julia had told Lucy, and Lucy had grinned. For all Joannie knew, Lucy didn't even know what a hot tub was.

Joannie wondered if she was teaching Lucy the wrong things, but she didn't think so. Her ex-husband embraced his poverty like it was a virtue. While Johnny finished cleaning the kitchen, Julia had begun talking about what they would eat that night for dinner and Lucy asked about lobster and Julia said sure. Lobster.

Joannie loved lobster.

They would go to the Fosters' to swim in their pool and eat lobster. And soak in the hot tub. Look up at the stars. Joannie assumed there would be stars.

Poor Johnny. She could imagine how he felt.

And so, Joannie realized, trying to rally herself, she should not sit on her couch and allow herself to grow sad. She needed to get out of her apartment as quickly as possible before she sabotaged her good fortune. She would leave her apartment the way she'd found it. She got up from the couch—an act of heroism—grabbed her small suitcase, and filled it with clothes, a bathing suit for each of them, Lucy's favorite stuffed animal, their toothbrushes, and then—a triumph—she was out of there. Piles of dust still on the floor. There was no time to vacuum, and besides that, the vacuum cleaner was broken.

"Goodbye, plants," she said.

There was a white SUV limo waiting in front of her building. They had come for her. The limo was ludicrous. Enormous. Gleaming in the sunlight. She thought of Willie Wonka, the golden ticket.

The back window opened, and there was Lucy.

"Mommy," Lucy called to her. "Get in!"

She would not get to say goodbye to Johnny. Thank him for his hospitality. They were on their way.

I will be okay, Joannie told herself, and then she opened the door.

Julia

I t was a fucking relief to get out of there.

That man, Johnny—a ridiculous nickname—was far inferior to Jonathan; he did not even know how not to look hurt when he learned that they were leaving. "But we had a good time, didn't we?" he had said, whispering in Julia's ear, much too intimate an act, after lunch, catching her alone. As if she might like to do it again. Julia didn't answer.

She did not want to be cruel, but she would be if forced. The whole morning-after vibe was humiliating, and besides that, her attention had shifted to Lucy. Lucy, who was sitting next to her on the plush leather seat of the enormous SUV Vivian had sent for them. Lucy was eating a mini Toblerone bar, breaking the bites off piece by piece. Beaming.

"I love these," Lucy said.

It was so easy to please a child.

She was also an easy child. A perfect child.

Joannie took the seat next to Jonathan, facing Julia and Lucy. Vivian had arranged for the limo instead of the Fosters' regular ride because Jonathan had told her that they were bringing guests. A mother, a little girl.

Joannie was looking out the window, as if the situation was too much for her to process. Suddenly, her head turned. "Are you wearing your seat belt?" she asked Lucy. None of them were. It was a limo, for fuck's sake. The car was a tank. Julia helped Lucy put on her seat belt. She put on her own, not wanting to seem like a hypocrite. Jonathan did not.

Jonathan asked her what she wanted to drink, and Joannie asked for seltzer. He gave her a small bottle of Pellegrino.

"Oh," she said. Joannie also looked happy, having been given her own individual bottle. It was as if she came from a third world country.

Julia wasn't sure, but it felt like there was a plan in place: to conquer and divide. She had Lucy. Jonathan had Joannie. She did not have to be jealous. Jonathan was going after Joannie for a variety of reasons. Julia was no fool. He was trying to make her jealous, something she would not fall for. Also this was payback. Sure. Fine. It didn't matter. Because really—and Julia had told him this once before—she didn't care who Jonathan slept with, as long as it wasn't Vivian.

Julia had taken her pill.

It only took fifteen minutes until her mind seemed sharp

again and she was able to focus. She was going home. She loved her house in the country. It was sleek and modern and clean. She had a barn for her horses. Her cats. She missed her cats. She would be home soon.

Looking across the limo, she was not entirely sure that she had made a fair trade. Jonathan had his earbuds in. His eyes were closed. Joannie was gazing out the window. Lucy was adorable and funny and smart, but it was hard work to make conversation for an entire drive. When the conversation lagged, Lucy looked at her expectantly.

"If there was anywhere you could go," she asked Lucy, "anywhere in the world, where would you want to go?"

"Hogwarts," Lucy said.

"Where is that?"

"Universal Studios," Lucy said. "There is a whole Harry Potter amusement park in Florida. My friend went. That is where I want to go."

"I want to go to Antarctica," Julia said.

"Antarctica?" Lucy asked. "Isn't it cold?"

"Sure, it's cold," she said. "But I have a feeling it would be magical. I want to see the emperor penguins. The polar bears. The icebergs. I want to see it all before Earth gets too warm, and it's all gone."

"Do you think that is going to happen?" Lucy said. "It won't really."

"It will," Julia said. "The temperature is steadily rising. There's no going back."

"No," Lucy said, tears springing to her eyes. "The scientists are going to fix it."

Clearly, Joannie had not been honest with this little girl.

Protecting her. Julia could traumatize this girl in less than the space of an hour. It was crazy to think she could raise a child. The girl was so pretty. She slipped her hand into Julia's, as if begging for reassurance.

"I think we should go to Harry Potter Land first," Julia said. "And then Antarctica, if you want to see the penguins."

Julia did not think children were allowed to travel to Antarctica.

Lucy clapped her hands. "Really?" she cried. "Harry Potter? Really?"

"Sure," Julia said. "Why not?"

"My classes are online," Lucy told her. "Maybe we can go now."

"Maybe," Julia said. "Why not?"

She thought about asking Joannie her opinion, but Joannie was still looking out the window. And in this way, Julia realized that she must be grateful to her, for talking to her daughter. It must be exhausting to be a parent around the clock. Julia had never properly considered that before.

"Can we go to Disney World, too?"

"Really?" Julia asked. This trip, unlike Antarctica, sounded a little bit like hell, but she remembered loving Disney World when she was a kid. There was a picture of her in her mother's office, a Polaroid, where she was hugging a life-size Goofy. The little girl Julia had loved it.

"My friend Nora went to both. They are right next to each other."

Julia felt an instant animosity toward Nora.

"Maybe," Julia said. "Let's talk to your mother about how

long we want to go for. No matter what, we can stay in a big suite and get room service."

"There are fireworks at Disney World."

Julia hated fireworks. They terrified her cats, all the local wildlife. The neighbors were always setting them off. Julia would have to educate Lucy. She also did not want this girl to grow up full of envy. It was important to have the things that other people had.

"I bet there are," Julia said.

"We're going to Hogwarts!" Lucy squealed.

Julia wondered how Joannie would feel, when she tuned back in. Lucy clapped her hands. She started bouncing in her seat.

Joannie turned her head; she saw Lucy smiling and she smiled, too. "Thank you," she mouthed to Julia. She had no idea, really, what she was thanking her for. Julia was going to bring Joannie with her on this vacation, a vacation that was at the bottom of the list of places Julia would ever want to go.

It was fine. Julia liked a good roller coaster. She liked to be scared out of her mind and then return to herself. Exhilarated.

Lucy

Lucy was so happy.

She was going to go to Universal Studios. To Hogwarts! Maybe this nice woman would buy her a wand. And candy. Lots and lots of candy. Lucy was not sure why, but she had a feeling this woman would buy her anything she asked for. She had pretty much said so.

Another time, there had been this other woman. Suzi. Suzi had been her dad's girlfriend for a long time and Suzi had been really nice and Suzi had loved her. Lucy loved Suzi, too, but she did not tell her mother this because she did not want her mother to be hurt. Sometimes her mother seemed sad, but mainly it was only when their apartment got messy. Or when

Lucy refused to do her online classes on Zoom. Or when it was one in the morning and Lucy could not fall asleep. Then, her mother would freak out.

Lucy hated that. Lucy did not want to make her mother unhappy, but she couldn't do online school for her. Her mom got upset with Lucy when she couldn't fall asleep, and that made everything worse. Her mom yelled at her, and then it was really impossible to sleep, so instead they would put on coats over their pajamas and go for a walk. Sometimes her mother stole flowers, but her mother said it wasn't bad stealing because she only took flowers from public spaces and not from people's yards.

Mainly her mother seemed fine.

The pandemic was hard and her mom wanted them to be happy, so she stopped making Lucy do school. "We're just going to get through this," she told her. "And we won't tell anyone about the flowers and the walks. Deal?"

Lucy agreed.

Her mother was always ordering them sushi, and they watched a lot of TV, more TV than anyone else she knew, and they took baths together. Lucy loved her mother more than she loved anyone else. More than she loved Suzi. More than she loved her dad. She did not like that her mother had kissed that man. Earlier that day by the pool, Lucy had broken them up. She could do that again if she had to. Even if he seemed nice.

It was okay for her father to have girlfriends, but really that wasn't okay, either. Because he had broken up with Suzi. Lucy missed her a lot, and that was not fair. The last time Lucy went to see her father, Suzi wasn't there and her dad hadn't planned anything for her visit and she was really bored and they ate a lot of frozen meals because her dad did not like to cook, and he said he was too broke to order takeout.

So probably it *was* okay for her dad to have girlfriends, if they were nice like Suzi, and she even wanted him to have another one. Really, she wanted her dad to get back together with Suzi, because she missed Suzi, but her dad had forbidden her to ever talk to Suzi again.

But it was not okay for her mom to have boyfriends. Ever.

Lucy did want to meet this woman's cats. Six cats. Lucy wanted to have six cats. She wanted to go down the waterslide on the man's boat. She wanted to go to Hogwarts!

The woman, Julia, seemed tired, and Lucy picked up on this because she kept saying "Mm-hmm," so Lucy stopped talking. She started shaking her leg, and Julia asked her to stop. She asked for something to eat, and there were chocolate mousse cups in the mini refrigerator. Julia let Lucy eat two. Her mom didn't seem to care. Her mom was looking out the window. Her mom seemed sad again, and Lucy was surprised, because there was going to be a swimming pool at the house, and her mom loved to swim.

Tyson had been really nice.

At first he'd seemed like just a stupid boy, but Lucy had had a good time at the sleepover, and she hoped that she would be allowed to sleep over again even if she had ended up sleeping with her mom because she got nervous down in the basement. She had kind of wanted to go to Tyson's soccer game, but she could tell that Julia really wanted to take her to her house, and Lucy knew that she could not have both; she had actually tried to see if they could go to the soccer game and then to her house, and since that wasn't possible, this was the better choice. Though the woman, Julia, made her nervous. She was so nice. Too nice. It made her think of Suzi. It had really been hard not being allowed to see Suzi again. She did not understand why. Her dad said mean things about Suzi. Things that could not be true. Sometimes he said mean things about Lucy's mom, too. Suzi had come to Lucy's school once, before school shut down. She had snuck onto the playground and given Lucy a present. It was a pillow that Suzi had sewn herself. Lucy did not understand why Suzi would give her a pillow.

"I can tell my mom that you were here, right?" Lucy had asked her. "My mom won't be mad. My mom likes you."

After Suzi and her dad broke up, Suzi came to their apartment. She brought her mom flowers and chocolate. Her mom gave her a hug. They laughed. They hugged each other again. But then everything changed. Her dad found out Suzi was seeing her at her mom's and the visits stopped.

"You can't tell your mom," Suzi said.

Suzi was crying. She told her that she was moving to Portland. Lucy did not know where that was, but Suzi had said Oregon, which Lucy knew was on the other side of the country, but not near her dad. Her dad lived in a farmhouse in Vermont with a bunch of other people. Hippies, her mother had said, as if *hippies* was a bad word. Her dad used to have long hair when she was a baby, but he had shaved it all off. It looked awful. Lucy thought hippies had long hair. How could he still be a hippie if his hair was short?

"I am going to keep sending you presents," Suzi told her. "And I have a new address and you can write me letters."

"I don't have stamps," Lucy told her, but Suzi pressed a book of stamps and a package of envelopes into her hands. And there were cat stickers, too. The envelopes already had Suzi's address on them, in Portland. Lucy truly believed that she would write her a letter, but she never did. Mainly, it was because she forgot. She also knew that it would make her dad angry. One time she thought of it and she went to look for the envelopes and they were gone.

It was weird to think about this.

Her whole life had seemed weird for a while now. It had been almost a year since she had been in school. Lucy used to love school. She got to see her friends there, and she was good at it. She was good at math. She was the fastest person in the class to get all the answers. She was faster than Oliver Bedrin, though the teacher treated him like he was a genius. She hoped that one day she would go back to school.

Jonathan

Jonathan was glad to be going home.

Basically, he did not like to leave it.

He had gotten too wealthy. Too successful. Everybody wanted something from him. So often—too often—he gave people things because it was easier that way. It basically cost him nothing, all the handouts, because he made money just by breathing. Every day, he woke up richer, but it was exhausting. He had people always telling him what to do next, how to get richer and richer, and he listened, because why not, but often he did not know why. Vivian once asked him what the money would mean if he were dead. "That makes no sense," he said.

She had strange ideas.

She was such a beautiful girl.

Woman. He remembered. Not a girl. A woman. An employee. Julia was so annoying, always watching him with her.

Still, strangely enough, he was at peace during the pandemic. If Julia had gotten pregnant according to plan, they would have had a baby to distract them during quarantine, but that had not happened. Jonathan had decided it was for the best. They had Vivian, after all.

He had said those exact words to Julia, and she had punched him.

But it was true.

Vivian was their Vietnamese orphan.

They both loved having her there. She distracted them. She was surprisingly good at Scrabble. She also did every last thing they did not want to do. She got someone into the house to clean the ducts, for Christ's sake. She was a fucking godsend. Julia was going to get over it, the baby. They could go to the shelter, get another fucking cat.

Then he had rented that goddamned hot air balloon.

He thought he knew what he was doing until he was up in the air and realized, when the wind started, that he didn't. He could not stop drifting. They could have died, but people died all the time. Better to laugh it off. Vivian had gotten people to take the hot air balloon out of the pool, and now he was going home with a little girl and the woman he had kissed as a teenager.

Believe it or not, he had not forgotten Joannie.

It had been his first kiss, too, and the next morning, he had looked for her at breakfast in the dining hall, but didn't see her. He sat at a table with his bunkmates and then all these pretty girls sat down with them, and that had been that. It was a gift that he had gotten to rediscover Joannie now. She had turned out to be interesting. She had published a novel. She had won awards for this novel, but she had never written anything else, she was divorced, and she had a child. She was basically ripe for saving.

Jonathan loved saving people.

He had saved Vivian. It did give him a feeling of ownership. "You're going to scare her away," Julia told him.

"You're the one who had her research Vietnamese babies," Jonathan said.

"True," Julia said. And then never mentioned it again. They stopped watching *Modern Family,* even though they had two seasons to go. Instead, Jonathan started taking trips into the city, visiting the office, having sex with other women.

It was driving Julia crazy now, his interest in Joannie.

It was Julia's fault. He could easily have left that house the night before and never given Joannie a second thought, because he was like that: ideas came in and out of his head. Joannie had rejected him, and that was that. But then Julia had fucked that man.

Jonathan had believed that they were happy. He had not learned, until the night before, the depth of Julia's unhappiness. Now, Jonathan did not know where they stood. At first he had thought that it might be war, but they were going home together, and war seemed foolish. Instead, they were bringing home some new friends. Joannie was lovely and she painted and Julia painted and they could paint together, and her little girl was cute and later that day they would take out the boat, which was something Jonathan always loved to do. He wanted to kiss Joannie again, too. And more.

Vivian was going to take care of everything. He had texted her, and she was in preparation mode. She was going to a toy store to have a present waiting for the girl and then to the farmers market, and she would have everything ready. Vivian. He had been gone for a day, and he missed her. As long as no one got cancer or got hit by a car or died in a hot air balloon accident, everything was going to be all right.

In the limo, Joannie leaned her leg against his. She had rejected him the night before but then realized the error of her ways. It was a relief. He was going to fuck her and then everything would be okay again.

Joannie

Joannie was almost as giddy as her daughter.

It was tentative, the giddiness. Because it seemed so easy and nothing was ever that easy. She had heard Julia offer Lucy a trip to Universal Studios and she had heard Lucy accept, without asking Joannie first.

In fact, something like this had already happened. Another woman growing attached to her daughter. For a short period of time, Joannie had befriended her ex-husband's ex-girlfriend. They shared jaw-dropping stories about their ex that only the two of them could properly understand. Suzi had shown up in town, and for a couple of weeks, she had stayed at their apartment, sleeping on the couch. Then Lucy told her dad about

Suzi. How she was staying with them, making banana pancakes in the morning, and that was the end of it. Joannie genuinely liked Suzi, but she was not worth it. Her ex-husband had gone ballistic, and that was never going to be part of her life again. So no more Suzi. She was not worth fighting for.

It was sad for Joannie to witness Lucy experiencing sadness and disappointment so early in life. Joannie wanted to shield Lucy from all sadness. But she could not control her ex-husband, or her ex-husband's ex-girlfriend. It was so unthinkable, all the disappointment Lucy was going to experience as she went through life. At eight years old, she already knew about loss, a broken heart. She was not allowed to see Suzi. Hopefully, Lucy would forget about her.

Joannie was looking out the window. This was her first ride in a limo. She had skipped her high school prom: the limo, the hotel, the whole experience. And while she knew that limos were bad for the environment, tacky, embarrassing, she had to admit that it was nice. The leather was crazy soft. She liked drinking her Pellegrino in a real glass while in a moving car, something she had never done before. She wanted her own mini Toblerone but was too embarrassed to ask.

Joannie knew how impressed she was by money. She understood how shallow her thoughts were. Her wants and desires. It almost seemed like she had been raised by wolves. Or in a foster home. She had had a perfectly fine, middle-class childhood.

It was adulthood that shocked her. Coming out of college, she appreciated for the first time what it meant to properly pay her own way. Rent, clothes, food, laptop computers, expensive bubble bath and skin care products. Everything.

For the rest of her life. It was a lot. She did not know how her parents had done it, bought a house, sent her to college. How everyone did it. It seemed impossible.

Somehow she was doing it, but not very well. Groceries had gotten so expensive, and Lucy loved raspberries, could eat them two packs at a time. It had gotten easier, actually, after Joannie got divorced. She made all the money, and she controlled all the money. She liked it that way. And she thought she was doing okay. She was doing it at least. She had sold the book. She wrote freelance. She taught writing. She was paying the rent, paying for everything. Until the pandemic, she had never carried a balance on her credit cards, paying it off each month, because she hated the idea of giving her money to a bank for literally nothing. Now it was going up, slow and steady, every month, the amount she owed, and Joannie set autopay to the lowest amount. She did not open her bank statements. Take-out sushi was the thing that provided happiness. She had given up therapy, after all.

The illusion of success—fuck success, the illusion of competence—crumbled when presented with the idea of a trip to Universal Studios. Lucy had begged. Numerous times. She told her that Suzi had promised to take her. Lucy's best friend, Nora, had gone. The thought of it brought Joannie to despair.

She pretended to hear nothing when she heard Lucy tell Julia that it would be her dream come true to go there. She looked out the window and hoped that the expression on her face remained blank.

"I am in the business of making dreams come true," Julia told Lucy. "That literally is my job."

That literally wasn't Julia's job.

She was, according to Wikipedia, actually a philanthropist. She ran the Foster Foundation. Usually, dream makers focused their attention on children who had cancer. Who were dying. Lucy was healthy. Lucy, though she might think otherwise, was a child of privilege. If Suzi had been her mother, Lucy would have been dressed in thrift-store clothes and survived on homeopathic medicine and lentils. Nonetheless, Joannie could not afford to take Lucy to Universal Studios, her daughter's ultimate dream. It was impossible. A debt she would not take on.

The conversation continued while Lucy told Julia every single thing she would do at Hogwarts. She knew all about it. The ride at Gringotts bank. The butterbeer. The things she wanted to buy. The train you took from the hotel. Joannie began to believe that Julia would make this happen. The good thing about online school was that Lucy would not miss any actual school. They could just get on an airplane and go. Joannie did not want to appear grateful, desperate, but she was so happy Lucy would get to go to Hogwarts when she was still a child.

Julia, unlike Suzi, was not a crazy person. But then again, why did Joannie assume that? Just her thinking it meant that Julia might actually be a crazy person. Two for two. It was really possible. Julia had cheated on her husband in the next room, and loudly. She did not have to be that loud. Joannie could feel the pressure of her leg against Jonathan's, and it felt illicit. It felt wonderful. It felt like a promise of something more. She had not had sex in years, and for the first time, she felt herself wanting to have it. She wondered if Julia noticed, her legs touching Jonathan's in the bright light of day, but she could not get herself to move her leg away.

She hoped that Julia understood that Joannie was also going to come on this trip. As much as Joannie, herself, did not actually want to go to Universal Studios. She could not have another Suzi story. That crazy fucking Suzi returned, right before the start of the pandemic, when the panic was just starting, when they were washing their hands compulsively and waiting for the announcement that school would be canceled. Suzi had shown up on the playground of Lucy's elementary school. The school had actually called the police when they realized that Suzi was not Lucy's mother, but recess was already long over when the police arrived. Suzi had given Lucy a present and hugged her goodbye. Joannie was grateful that was all it was.

Don't worry, Suzi had written in a letter taped to the front door of their apartment that same day. *I am not upset with you, my bodhi warrior, but you don't have to protect Lucy from me. I am her other mother. I love her. I love you both. This is not the end of our journey together.*

That was the end of Suzi.

Joannie was surprised that her thoughts had drifted to Suzi. Julia and Jonathan might be complicated, but they were not going to cause her that kind of pain. She would take what she could get, and they were offering her the moon.

⟶

Johnny's pool was nice. The Fosters' pool was almost otherworldly. The French doors in the kitchen opened up to an enormous lawn and then the infinity pool, which was perched at the end of a rocky beach. The bay. Not the ocean, but still a private expanse of water. The pool had a gorgeous tiled floor. The hot tub. And flowers. There were so many flowers, potted in blue ceramic vases and growing in flower beds.

"I love your flowers," Joannie told Jonathan, who seemed surprised, as if he had never noticed them before.

"A landscaper," Julia said, as if somehow, therefore, the flowers did not count or were rendered invisible. The flowers were beautiful. If Joannie were ever to own a house, she would plant her own flowers. She dreamed of planting her own flowers.

And there were the cats—so many cats—Julia's cats, and also feral cats that came for the bowls of cat food left outside, and Lucy had looked as happy as Joannie had ever seen her. Joannie wondered about the expression on her own face. She was trying so hard to be cool. In the limo, she had had an overwhelming urge to cry. Now she was giddy; she could feel herself almost bouncing out of her skin. She hoped that they would not have to go to Universal Studios right away, because she did not want to leave this house. She was excited for her lobster.

"It's nice, right?" Jonathan said.

"I love it here," Joannie said, and immediately realized her mistake. This was not her house to love. She was not playing it cool.

After Joannie and Lucy petted the cats, they went for a swim in the big, beautiful pool. Both Julia and Jonathan said that it was too cold for them, which was absurd, because the pool was heated. Joannie felt self-conscious in an actual bathing suit this time, giving both Jonathan and Julia a chance to see her body, but she was not self-conscious enough to not go swimming.

Somehow, every swim still felt like the last. The year before, in the heart of the pandemic, the town only let you swim in two-hour shifts, and limited the number of swimmers allowed in, and removed all the plastic lounge chairs, so it almost felt like a pool prisonscape. Julia had loved it anyway.

It was not even Memorial Day weekend. It would be another month before the town even opened the pool, hopefully with fewer restrictions. Rich people never thought about that, how much more time they had in their swimming pools. They could open them in April, close them in November, swim in the middle of the night if they felt like it. Swim naked. This very well might be the only time Joannie and Lucy ever had the chance to swim in the Fosters' pool. In Joannie's experience, invitations to return to a place were rarely forthcoming.

Joannie was not prepared when Vivian emerged from the house. Somehow, it had not occurred to her that she would meet Jonathan's prized assistant. She might have gasped, but she quickly covered her mouth with her hand. Vivian brought out a tray of fresh lemonade and cheese and crackers. She was exquisite.

"I love cheese!" Lucy cried.

"I'm so glad," Vivian said.

Joannie felt herself blushing. She felt guilty that she and Lucy had created work for her. This beautiful young woman was not a waitress, but she also was.

"I have presents," Vivian said. Her voice was quiet and clear.

"For me?" Lucy said. "Why?"

"Yes, for you," Vivian said. "Jonathan and Julia want you to feel comfortable."

Lucy looked at Joannie to see if it was okay. What wasn't okay at this point? Lucy rushed out of the pool. Vivian had picked out an extremely soft stuffed cat that Lucy hugged to her chest, and then she handed her three small metal containers of putty. Lucy loved putty. Somehow, without having been told, Vivian knew that her daughter loved putty.

"Look, Mom!" Lucy shouted. "Putty!"

"I see," Joannie said with a wan smile.

Joannie felt sad, a small pang that Vivian had not bought a present for her. Joannie wished she did not feel this way. She hated that she allowed herself to be constantly disappointed. It was also incredibly nice in the pool. Joannie did not get out. She watched as Lucy went to the table and started to eat the cheese, standing up, as if she had been starved. Vivian put her hand on Lucy's head and then removed it. She was wearing a white T-shirt, khaki shorts.

"I'm sorry," Vivian said. "But are you Joannie Nelson?"

Joannie's jaw dropped. She had never been recognized before.

"You know her?" Jonathan asked.

"Of course," Vivian said. "She's a writer. She wrote one of my favorite books."

"It was good?" Julia asked, sounding surprised.

"Of course it was good," Jonathan said.

Joannie knew that she had to respond. She did not know what to say. "Thank you," she said. "I don't know what to say."

This was the kind of moment she lived for, and she had blown it. Joannie felt herself wanting to disappear.

"Are you working on anything new?" Vivian asked.

Joannie shook her head. Now she wanted to die.

"It's been hard," she said. "The pandemic. No childcare. I can't believe you read my book."

"I mean, I didn't just read it," Vivian said. "I loved it. I've read it more than once. It was taught in my freshman English class."

"Wow," Joannie said. She had never felt less articulate. She had heard this before, but it had been years. Her book wasn't on the shelves of bookstores anymore. Joannie sometimes wondered, while editing bad novels for money, if she actually existed. Rather than basking in Vivian's praise, she was ashamed not to be writing another book.

"Join us, Vivian," Julia said.

"Oh no," Vivian said. "You have guests."

"That's okay," Joannie said, mortified.

"I have work to do," Vivian insisted.

She appeared to be as embarrassed as Joannie. Joannie wondered how she must seem to her. Swimming in the Fosters' pool, eating the free cheese. She must appear to be the freeloader that she actually was.

"Take the rest of the day off," Jonathan said.

"I have the arrangements to make. Right, Julia? Universal Studios. Hotel. Flights."

"Yay!" Lucy cried. "We're really going. Hogwarts?"

"Why not?" Julia said. "Do you want to leave tonight?"

"Tonight?" Joannie cried. She could hear the distress in her voice. Joannie wanted to stay at this house. She had been promised lobster. At the same time, she also very much wanted to go home, back to her small apartment. It was irrational, she knew. She also did not know if she was crazy to go along with this. How could she trust these people? Jonathan had already hurt her once before. Julia had snapped at her over breakfast about her drawing.

Joannie knew better.

They had to have better things to do than take a single mother and her daughter to Universal Studios. It also made no sense. But so what? Lucy had stopped doing her work in online school months ago. Imagine flunking out of the third grade. They would figure it out. They could go to Universal Studios or they could continue to sit in their apartment, day after day after day, feeling bored and afraid and very much alone in the world. Was there a choice? It had been a very long year.

Joannie looked at Lucy. She would be furious if she was not allowed to go. Her daughter looked back at her, somehow aware that a decision was being made. She had learned to recognize panic in her mother's face. She was clearly caught between emotions. Lucy cut off a large piece of Brie and ate it without a cracker.

"I want lobster first," Lucy said. "For dinner. Right, Mommy? I want to go tomorrow."

"I bought the lobster," Vivian said.

"Do you see what I am talking about?" Jonathan said. "Vivian bought the lobster."

"Well then," Julia said. "How about tomorrow?"

"I'll book the tickets," Vivian said.

"Jonathan?" Julia said. "You're coming?"

"I have some things," Jonathan said.

Things, of course, was so vague. Things. He did not want to be with her. Joannie had thought he wanted to be with her—their legs touching in the limo had seemed electric—but she was wrong. "But you should all go," Jonathan said. "Enjoy yourselves. Truly."

"Seriously?" Julia said.

Joannie also wanted to protest, but she knew better.

"Really?" Lucy asked. "We can go tomorrow? I'm so excited."

"For how long?" Vivian asked.

"Three days?" Julia said. "Four?"

"Four!" Lucy said.

"Three." Julia nodded.

"Got it," Vivian said.

Joannie said nothing. Vivian had loved her book. Now she was making travel arrangements for them. Jonathan did not want her after all. She had misread the signs. They both looked so good to her, effortlessly attractive. Julia, she did not understand. In the last two days, Joannie and Lucy had become a charity case. Joannie had once had high hopes for herself. Now she found herself wanting, once again, people she could not have. It was humiliating.

Vivian started walking away backward.

"Have a lovely day," she said. "I'm so pleased to have met you. I can't wait to read your next book."

Next book. There was no next book. Now Julia really wanted to go home. She sank under the water and held her breath. She realized only then why this pool was so especially wonderful. It was a saltwater pool. The water actually felt gentle. She could live in this swimming pool. When Joannie finally came up for air, Vivian was gone.

"I am going to swim some laps," Joannie said.

There was nothing else she could do. Dying was not an option. She was a mother. She took three strokes and breathed, then took three more strokes, lifting her head to the other side, and breathed again. It felt effortless, gliding through the water. She had been waiting for this. She had wondered, day in and day out, during the never-ending quarantine, a year without school, if they would ever, ever make it out. Joannie swam one lap and then another, and then, unbidden, an idea came to her. An actual idea. A sentence fully written in her mind. Joannie could not remember the last time she had had an idea.

Lucy was asleep on the bed, sprawled out in the middle, legs spread one way, arms the other. Joannie was pressed all the way against the edge, about to fall off. Plus, the pillows were too firm. With two pillows, her head was too high, and with just one, too low. She would never fall asleep. She would feel terrible the next day from having not slept, and then she would have to travel, something that made her nervous already, her first time since the pandemic, and how could she take her daughter to a crowded theme park on only a couple of hours' sleep? She couldn't, she couldn't do it.

She kept thinking that she should not go, that they should not take this trip. They should not go. They should not go. It did not matter if Lucy was upset with her. It did not matter if Lucy was heartbroken. They should not go. They shouldn't go. Because Joannie didn't want to. More than anything, she did not want to go. She did not want to go to an airport during a pandemic even if the pandemic was sort of over and they would be safe wearing masks on the plane. She did not want to go to Universal Studios. She hated everything about theme parks. She hated rides. She hated lines. She hated crowds. She hated other people. She hated that Jonathan had kissed her and that she had liked it. She hated that she now wanted something more to happen and it wouldn't. In the morning, she would be on a plane. Except she couldn't get on a plane. Joannie couldn't sleep. She couldn't sleep. Her heart was racing.

She took an Ativan.

She tried to meditate. She hated meditating.

Then it was two in the morning.

At three in the morning, Joannie heard footsteps outside her door. She didn't hesitate, just got out of bed and went to see who was there, because she had to talk to whoever was awake—Jonathan, Julia, even Vivian, it didn't matter who—and explain why the trip had to be canceled. They had to figure out a plan before Lucy woke up. There would be some story they could tell her. They could tell Lucy that the numbers were up, that the virus rate was higher in Florida than anywhere else in the country, and that would be that. Lucy would be sad. Too bad, kiddo. Too fucking bad.

It was Jonathan in the hallway. In striped pajama bottoms and a white T-shirt. He was so handsome, the way rich people sometimes were. There was a perfection to him, an ideal beauty. He did want her. He had to. Why else was he there? That seemed beside the point.

"I can't go," she told him. "I can't go to Universal Studios. I have to tell Julia."

Jonathan put his fingers to her lips.

"You're panicking," he said. "It will be okay. It will be okay. Take a deep breath."

"I can't go."

Joannie was actually panicking. The Ativan hadn't done a thing. She was not even the littlest bit calm. It was crazy, to be that worried about doing something that she desperately wanted to do for her daughter.

"Let me tuck you in," he said. "You'll sleep. You must be so tired. You'll feel better in the morning. Everything always seems better in the morning."

Joannie shook her head.

Jonathan took her hand. "I'll tuck you in."

It was preposterous, the very idea of Jonathan putting Joannie to bed, tucking her in, but she also thought it was nice. To be taken care of. Tucked in.

"How is the room?" he whispered.

"It's beautiful," Joannie said.

It was. It had a view of the water. She would not complain about the pillows. They went inside. Lucy was still sprawled out on the bed. It looked like there was less room than before, if that was even possible.

"I want to kiss you," Jonathan whispered, and Joannie nodded. She felt past surprise. The night before, she had been so grateful when Lucy came into the room and made it easy to refuse him. The night before, she had had absolutely no interest in him, and it was better that way. Now she very much wanted to kiss him.

"We can't," she said. "Here."

But Jonathan looked at her like he still wanted to, *there,* and she wondered if she would ever have this chance again. She had begun to think she would never be loved by anyone who was not Lucy. She had made her peace with that, but now life had provided her with a chance that she actually wanted to take. And so they kissed, even though Joannie had just said they couldn't. And somehow, the kiss calmed her down. It was a long, slow, calming kiss. An amazing kiss. Her heart had stopped racing. She pulled away and looked at her sleeping daughter.

She could do this. She could take Lucy to Universal Studios, not break her daughter's heart. The last thing she wanted to do was break her daughter's heart. She could fall asleep. Four hours of sleep was better than no hours of sleep. Jonathan kissed her again. Jonathan Foster was a very good kisser. The kissing continued, going from calm to urgent, making it harder and harder for Joannie to even worry about Universal Studios. It had been so long since she had been kissed like this. The last time she had had sex it had been with her husband and she had despised him, but she had slept with him anyway because it made things easier, and that was how she lived for a while.

"We have to be quiet," she said.

She said this. Joannie. Not Jonathan Foster. She put her

hand down his pajama bottoms. She slid them off of his ass. She remembered how to do these things.

"There," she said, pointing to an ottoman in front of the window. Because she had not entirely lost her mind, she would not have sex on the bed where Lucy slept, not that there was room anyway.

She sat down on the ottoman—it was a beautiful ottoman, red patterned silk—and Jonathan followed her, and he pulled down Joannie's pajama bottoms, and she guided him inside her. This, Joannie knew, was the stupidest but also maybe the most exciting thing she had done in a long time.

When they were done, she turned onto her side and he held her in his arms, her breasts pressed against his chest. Their calves and feet were suspended in midair, but somehow they made it work. She could feel his heart beat. She worried that he was uncomfortable. "I love you," she whispered.

Somehow, it just slipped out.

"You're sweet," he said, and Joannie understood her mistake.

"Get back into bed," he said. "If you can."

Lucy had turned onto her side. There was room.

"Sleep," he said. "We'll talk in the morning."

Lucy had slept through the entire thing. Joannie wondered why the room wasn't dark and she realized that there was a full moon, its brightness streaming in.

She watched as Jonathan Foster closed the curtains. Joannie did as she was instructed, getting back into bed, because she did not know what else to do. She thought Jonathan would kiss her again, and he did, this time on the forehead, like a proper tuck-in.

"You tucked me in," she said with a smile.

"Sleep tight," he said.

It was almost as if nothing had happened.

Had anything happened?

Joannie still could not sleep after he left. She was filled with new anxiety, self-loathing. Tears slid silently down her cheeks, and she prayed for sleep even though there was nothing that Joannie actually believed in. She gave up, because it was pointless—there was so little time left, why bother even trying to sleep?—but she must have slept, because there was Lucy, jumping on top of her.

"Wake up, wake up, wake up!" she called out. "We're going to Hogwarts. We're going to Hogwarts."

Vivian

Vivian couldn't sleep.

It got later and later.

She had taken an anxiety pill and still didn't sleep. That had never happened before. She wondered if she should take two, but she did not want to be that person. This job was ruining her.

She had read Joannie's book. She had read and reread it. She loved it. It was a book she gave to friends. It was the kind of book that she wanted to write one day. Vivian hated that Joannie Nelson was at the Fosters' house. It was soul-crushing to take in her obsequious good manners, her longing visible on her face, her appreciation heartbreaking. It ruined everything for Vivian. Her idea of what it meant to be a successful writer.

Joannie's desperation was painful to watch.

She was so grateful for everything.

To swim in the pool.

A few tins of putty for her daughter and some Brie.

Lobster.

She was pathetic, really.

And if Joannie Nelson was pathetic, what did that make Vivian Smith? She wanted to be a star. She had gone to an elite college. She had had dreams. She was twenty-four years old, and her life was completely stalled. She was a personal assistant. It felt like she was back in that sad room under the stairs, only it was a very big room with nice furniture. So what?

At three in the morning, Vivian watched Jonathan Foster have sex with Joannie, her former writer crush, on an ottoman while Joannie's daughter slept only a few feet away. Joannie couldn't know that there were cameras in every room of the house. Vivian sometimes watched the monitors when she was bored. She had watched, for instance, Jonathan Foster masturbate in front of the living room window, completely naked. Like he was a god or something. She watched Julia play with the cats, talk to them. Profess her undying love. To her cats. In a high-pitched voice no human would ever be allowed to hear. Really, they were both boring. That was the basic truth. Usually there was nothing to see.

Joannie shook while having sex with Jonathan. Her head was tilted back. Her eyes were wide open. She had her hands on Jonathan's shoulders, gripping him. Her fingers would probably leave marks. Her daughter was *in the room*. It was so wrong. So wrong. What if the girl woke up, saw her mother like that? What would she think? She would be scarred for life. Poor fucking kid.

Vivian watched Joannie quiver. There was something so erotic about how quiet they were. Vivian touched herself, watching. She was disgusted. With Joannie. With herself. She was jealous. She was turned on. She came at the same time as Joannie. It had been two years since she'd had sex.

Vivian realized that she was no better than Julia, jealous of all those women Jonathan was fucking. She had been the one to tip off Page Six about Jonathan and the TV actress. She had wanted Julia to know. She had not wanted to tell her. Vivian had thought Julia would end the marriage and was disappointed when nothing happened. She had thought Julia was a strong woman. She was wrong.

Jonathan Foster was beautiful. Too beautiful for a man. All those times she had watched him, naked, pleasuring himself. Jonathan had told her that she was beautiful once and she had returned the compliment. "You are beautiful, too," she had said, looking down.

He had patted her on the head, like she was a little girl.

She felt like she was ten years old.

The next day, Julia informed them that the word was off-limits.

Jonathan had laughed.

"*Beautiful?* It's not a curse," he said. "Can we still say *fuck?*"

"And *shit* and *damn,*" Julia responded.

Vivian understood.

Julia was telling Jonathan that she, Vivian, was off-limits.

Joannie clung to Jonathan when the sex was over, but this

state of bliss would be over soon. They were going to break that ottoman, and then it would be Vivian's job to have it fixed. It was all so mortifying. One of her favorite writers, reduced like that, to Jell-O. This woman was going to let the Fosters pay for her vacation, buy her daughter's affection with presents and a trip, ironically enough, to Harry Potter Land. She had no integrity. No spine. She had never written a second book. It had been years. Vivian checked periodically. This woman was a goddamned cautionary tale. Vivian was going to write. She was done with this job. This weird life. She would go to graduate school. In just two years, she had saved enough to pay her tuition in full. She would never be that needy. She thought of her own mother, her real mother, back in Vietnam, who couldn't afford to keep her.

"You are pathetic," Vivian said to the black-and-white screen. She watched Jonathan kiss Joannie on her forehead and then leave the room. Lucy slept through the whole thing. Vivian could not be sure, because the footage was grainy, but it looked like Joannie had begun to cry, lying flat on her back, a thin straight line all the way at the edge of the bed. Vivian had wondered what it would be like to have sex with Jonathan Foster. And now she knew.

It was time to go.

Julia

Lucy woke up bouncing and ready to go. Joannie looked like she had been hit over the head with a sledgehammer. Circles under her eyes. Pale. Twitchy, even. Vivian ordered the car, a regular sedan this time, and they got in and were on their way.

Julia would regret it.

She already regretted it.

She was on a vacation with two essential strangers to a place that she detested, in a land filled with germs. This had not occurred to Julia when she decided to take Lucy on her dream vacation: how much she herself would hate it there. A pretty big oversight. Julia thought money could make any place palatable, but this wasn't true. It was the middle of May and somehow already 95 degrees and there they were, out in the blazing sun. They bought sun hats at the airport. Sun hats did not help.

If anything, this was a crash course against parenting. She was going to get the idea out of her system. For once and for all. Of course Jonathan didn't come. He knew that he was going to hate it there. He never did anything he did not want to do. What, he would say, is the point of being rich?

It was one thing that he chose not to come. Only he did not warn her, stop her—that was the biggest betrayal. He listened to her make plans with Lucy while he pressed his leg against Joannie's, acting as if she could not see them, as if they were not right in front of her. He had let her go, knowing how much she would hate it. He did not give her Vivian. He put her in the car and closed the door goodbye. *Goodbye, Julia. Goodbye, Joannie. Goodbye, little girl.*

"My assistant," he reminded her when she asked to bring Vivian. As if he owned her. As if she did not spend half of her time doing things for Julia. This was not the first time Julia had had an idea and gone with it without thinking it through.

Diagon Alley had been re-created. It was as if they were in nineteenth-century London—a cobblestoned street, old-timey signs, dragons perched on the tops of buildings—but everything had a candy-colored sheen, orange shutters that were way too bright, and Julia felt claustrophobic, surrounded by streaming children and bearded wizards roving the grounds. Rides had changed since she was a kid. There was a roller coaster that they went on called the Hagrid, all of them crammed into motorcycle seats, and while Julia remembered loving roller coasters as a child, this was next level. Julia had vomited in her mouth and swallowed it down. Because she was strapped into her fake motorcycle, immobile. She had never been so terrified.

Lucy held her hand and screamed. Thrilled.

Joannie had known better. Which was also maddening. She did not get on the roller coaster. In fact, she went on *none* of the rides. She did not inform Julia until they were already on the airplane that she categorically did not go on rides. Fuck her for that. She was the mother. She had to go on the rides.

But that was what Julia was for. The money was not enough. Lucy was happy, and maybe that was something. It was nice to squeeze the girl's hand, scream together, talk about the rides after—they were in a club her mother was not in. But the Hagrid was too much. The roller coaster had taken everything out of her.

Stepping off the fake motorcycle, her legs wobbly, her mouth tasting of vomit, Julia noticed that at least Joannie looked equally miserable. Julia was glad. Julia was done. She was out. She had gone on many, many rides, been turned upside down and spun around. She had lasted hours. Vivian had signed her up for a VIP tour guide and so they got to skip all the lines and even take a little cart from one ride to another, but it did not make the day less hot or the screaming children less awful. Even at the front of the line, she and Lucy still had to wait for one ride to end before getting on the next. "Do you know how rich I am?" she asked one of the security guards who told her he could not speed up the process. He seemed thrilled to not be able to help her. Julia hated it when she acted like an asshole. A day at Hogwarts brought it out.

"I'm going back to the hotel," she told Joannie, squeezing her hand, as if to give her strength. "You two have a good time."

Julia could see the panic on Joannie's face. It had seemed possible that Julia and Joannie could be friends. She hated theme parks as much as Julia did. She liked to draw. She clearly hated the general population as much as Julia did. But she was useless to travel with. Joannie had told Lucy that the butterbeer was disgusting, disappointing the girl. She could barely fake a smile. Lucy was fine, but neither Julia nor Joannie was having a good time. It was a question of who was having a worse time.

"Don't go!" Joannie cried, grabbing her hand and not letting go. "Please."

Lucy's face was bright red. She looked like she was about to pass out, but she also wouldn't stop moving, rushing from ride to ride, wanting to do everything, buy everything. Julia had bought Lucy everything she had asked for, and they all took turns carrying the shopping bags. Lucy insisted on wearing the Gryffindor scarf and cape, even though it was over ninety degrees outside. Joannie told her she was going to die of heat exhaustion and Lucy would not listen. Up until then, until this place, Hogwarts, she had seemed like a lovely little girl. Maybe it turned children into goblins.

"Don't leave!" Lucy cried. "Please don't leave!"

They had both grown attached to her. Sure, that was nice. That was not enough. She was nobody's fairy godmother.

"I'm sorry," she said, shaking her head. "There's an air-conditioned hotel room waiting for me."

Julia was not the mother. She did not want to be the mother; she was grateful not to be a mother if it meant that she had to go to places like Universal Studios. Be responsible for a child nonstop, all day. Her mind was being blown by how quickly she was giving up on the idea of something she had tried so hard to obtain. Motherhood.

She was stunned by how much work Lucy was, and this was not even a baby. Not even a toddler. Eight years old. Could walk and talk and go to the bathroom on her own. Still, she needed to be taken to the bathroom. She needed to be dressed appropriately. She needed sunblock applied to her because she could not be trusted to apply it on her own. She had to be told not to sit backward on rides. Not to leave garbage on tables. To wipe her face. To wash her hands. To stop running. To drink water. She did not even listen or do half the things that she was told. Julia wanted to tell Joannie to stop telling her daughter to do things, it was so unpleasant to listen to, but really, almost all of Joannie's instructions made sense.

"Stay," Joannie begged. "A little longer."

"I'm sorry," Julia said. "I can't."

"One more ride!" Lucy cried.

Julia had bankrolled this trip. That had to be enough. She reached into her bag, found her wallet, and handed Joannie a credit card. "Use it for anything."

"Another wand!" Lucy cried.

"You don't need another wand," Joannie said, not accepting the credit card. "Goddamn it. You already have two, which is one too many."

And there it was, that awful mother voice. The voice of her own mother, of all mothers. Disapproving and mean. Of course Lucy did not need another wand, but she should have one. Clearly, this was going to be the only time she was ever taken to Universal Studios. But Julia was done. Done and done. Lucy started to cry.

"Don't cry," Julia said. This was not the point of the trip.

This made Lucy cry harder.

"You know what? We're going to go back with you," Joannie said. "I think that makes the most sense. I'm exhausted. My head is pounding. We've gotten too much sun."

"No!" Lucy cried.

Lucy looked back and forth from Joannie to Julia, realizing that they were really going to make her leave. She had arrived at the best place on earth, and they were taking her away.

Julia saw a strange look in the girl's eyes, and then, just like that, Lucy bolted. Julia stared, almost paralyzed, as Joannie took off after her, a beat too late but still running. The VIP handler had been looking at his phone, oblivious.

"Fuck," Julia said. "Motherfuck."

Lucy

The hotel swimming pool was full of people. Lucy sat next to her mother on the one available lounge chair, but she refused to get in. Her mother had told her it would be nice to be back at the pool. To go for a swim and cool off.

"I don't like it here," Lucy said. "I want to go home."

All of her cuts and bruises had been cleaned up. Her nose had bled all over her new Hermione T-shirt, but a doctor at the park told her it was fine and recommended icing it. She was sure that her nose was broken, but the doctor told her it wasn't broken. Nothing was broken. The palms of her hands stung. It hurt so much, but everyone told her she was fine. Lucy would never run away again. She felt humiliated. She had

lost one of her new stuffed animals. Julia said she would buy
her another, but Lucy was ashamed of her outburst—she had
never had one before—and so she told Julia that she did not
want the replacement stuffie, even though she did.

Lucy just wanted to go home. She had had fun with her new
friend Tyson. He had a pool. He had a huge TV in the basement. He had a nice dad who made her lots of delicious bacon.
Maybe, and she knew that it was stupid, he could be her other
dad. Like Suzi had been her other mother. She liked him much
more than Jonathan, and besides that, she just wanted to go
home. She had looked for Suzi at Hogwarts, because Suzi had
promised once to take Lucy there, but she wasn't there. She
had always sort of believed that Suzi had special powers, but
she didn't.

No one did.

Harry Potter was a character in a book. She had hoped to
see him at Universal Studios, but there were only posters and
sculptures and pictures from the movies.

She begged her mother to take her home.

"Please," she cried.

She was embarrassed to be crying at a hotel swimming
pool. She wanted to stay in her room, which was cool, air-
conditioned, but her mother had insisted. Her mother always
wanted to go to the pool.

Lucy's knees hurt. The palms of her hands hurt. She was
sunburned, and her mom had put lots of sunblock on her, so
it was completely unfair that that had happened, too. Her
mother held her close, which made Lucy feel hot. Julia had
stayed in her room. Julia did not seem to like her as much
as she had the day before, and that was confusing, too. Her

mother had told her once that no one could be unhappy in a swimming pool, but she was wrong. Lucy hated when her mother was wrong. "It's going to make all my Band-Aids come off if I go in," she said.

"I can put on new Band-Aids," Joannie said.

Lucy shook her head. "I want to go back to the room, and then I want to go home."

She looked at her mother looking at the pool. They were supposed to stay two more days. "You can go in," Lucy said. "If you have to."

Her mother shook her head, still gazing at the swimming pool. Lucy had not meant her offer, and hopefully her mother understood that. "Let's go back to the room. And then let's go home."

"Really?"

"Let me talk to Julia," she said. "She bought the plane tickets. I don't want to offend her."

"Please," Lucy begged.

Her mom sighed. "I want to go home, too."

They left the pool and walked through the lobby and got into the elevator, and then got out of the elevator and walked down a long, long hallway. It was exhausting, just getting from one place to another. Lucy had not known a hotel could be this big.

Her mom wanted to go home, too. Lucy was not surprised. She could see it in her mother's eyes, on the crowded train to Hogwarts, a panic that she was trying to keep inside. Lucy knew her mother. Lucy knew that her mother did not actually want to come on this trip, but that she had come for her. This was the kind of trip to take with her dad, who would go on all the rides, but her dad was too poor. She was still glad that she had come. The rides had been amazing. Julia had bought her the best stuff. Julia went with her on all the rides. Lucy would tell Nora all about it.

"Good," Lucy said. "We'll go home. I want to text Tyson."

"Tyson?"

"From the sleepover." Lucy could not believe that her mom had forgotten who Tyson was.

They got back to the room and her mom collapsed on the bed. Lucy lay down next to her.

"Are you sure, bunny rabbit?" her mom asked her. "About going home? You wanted to come here so badly."

"I went to Harry Potter. It was fun. I got two wands. I drank butterbeer and went on so many rides. I did everything I wanted to do. The Hagrid was crazy. Now I want to go home. Please, Mommy."

"But you're glad we came?" her mother asked, squeezing her hand.

"I'm glad we came."

Lucy knew that this was the right answer. Mainly, it was true. Her life had become so weird, like just in the last day, and it was confusing. Staying at that house with those rich people. Why were they there? Were they secretly related? Her mom had once taken her to a fancy house in someplace called the Hamptons. Her mom had said the woman who owned the house was a close family friend and loved them dearly, but they had never gone back.

Joannie

Joannie felt embarrassed, telling Julia that they wanted to leave. It seemed wrong that they could not stick it out. She also did not want to seem ungrateful. This, of course, was one of the problems of accepting gifts from people. Becoming beholden. Was she beholden to Julia and Jonathan Foster? She had had sex with Jonathan in the middle of the night and then, the next day, she found herself flying first-class for the first time, sitting next to Julia and realizing that she had not only made a mistake, she had done a wrong thing. Immoral. Even if Julia had been the one to suggest a partner swap. Julia and Jonathan Foster were married. Joannie was a terrible person. Julia would be hurt. Or would she?

Joannie had no idea. But Julia had every right to feel hurt. Joannie wanted to take the sex back. Because now, after, she found herself wanting impossible things. She wanted to be loved. She wanted to live in that house with the view of the water. She wanted Jonathan and Julia Foster to take care of her, but Jonathan hadn't even come to Universal Studios. He did not come down for breakfast or ride with them to the airport. Julia had been ready to abandon her at the theme park. Joannie wanted them to be more. To care about her. Really and truly. Had the Fosters made actual promises? Because she felt as alone as ever. There was, for instance, never going to be a reward.

In the hotel room, Lucy watched TV and Joannie went on the Internet, and there were flights leaving that night, flights leaving the next morning. Could she change the flights or would she have to buy new tickets? Joannie did not know what to do.

All day, Joannie had felt awkward talking to Julia because she had had sex with Jonathan. Really, she already felt awkward talking to Julia. She had wanted Julia to like her and she did not think there was any reason for Julia to like her and it was clear that Julia was smitten with her very adorable daughter, and this played into Joannie's long-held theory about herself, which was that she had once been an interesting, appealing person, but she no longer was, but at least she was Lucy's mother, and Lucy was a very appealing girl.

Joannie did not buy plane tickets.

"I don't know what to do," she said out loud.

She had this idea that she could ask Vivian. But she had

the distinct feeling that Vivian did not like her. That Vivian thought she was a loser. Vivian had loved her book and now look at her, a disappointment. A cautionary tale. A loser. It was true; Joannie was disgusted by herself.

She looked at Lucy, happily watching TV in bed.

"Could you turn it down?" she asked Lucy.

Everything was always so loud. Even her daughter, a constant source of noise. Joannie realized that Lucy had fallen asleep. Joannie muted the sound on the TV. She would not turn it off, for fear of waking her.

Joannie texted Julia in the hotel room next door.

JOANNIE: Hey. We want to leave early. Would that be okay?

JULIA: Thank God.

JOANNIE: Tonight? Tomorrow?

JULIA: Let's go tomorrow. Eat dinner. No rush. I'll book the tickets.

JOANNIE: I can pay you.

JULIA: Don't be ridiculous.

JOANNIE: What about Jonathan? He was going to join us?

JULIA: Changed his mind. Let's get the fuck out of here.

JOANNIE: Thank you!!!!!

JULIA: No, thank you!!!!! Is Lucy okay?

JOANNIE: She's fine. She's tired. I think she had fun. She did. Before she fell.

JULIA: Let's meet for dinner.

They would go out for dinner. They would go to sleep. They would go home. Joannie sighed. She was so relieved.

She always got carried away. The night before—before Jonathan, and then after Jonathan—she had felt overwhelmed, filled with worry, so panicked she almost wanted to die. Now she was in a hotel room. It was another wonderful bed, with a wonderful mattress and very crisp sheets, and Lucy—a girl who never napped—snored and held on tightly to her arm, and Joannie fell asleep, too. The last thing she told herself before drifting out of consciousness was that she could buy herself a new bed. Maybe before the couch.

Joannie was not sure where she was when she woke up. Less than an hour had passed. Lucy was next to her on the bed, back to watching TV.

"Where are we?" she said.

"The hotel," Lucy answered. "Florida."

Joannie nodded. She remembered.

"Are we going home?" Lucy asked her.

"Tomorrow," Joannie said. "Tomorrow."

Jonathan

Jonathan realized that he was not going to join them at Universal Studios. He had told Julia that he might to placate her. But who was he kidding?

Even if he ever was to become a father, he would not subject himself to such a place. If totally necessary, he would rent a theme park for the day. He did not think that would actually be possible, at least not one of the major ones. There were some things that money could not and probably should not buy. Maybe in another country, in Qatar or somewhere in Latin America, or even in the Midwest, there was a failing amusement park he could rent. Vivian could do the research. But he also did not want to die on a decrepit roller coaster.

Fortunately, it was not an issue, because they were all on a plane to Universal Studios without him. Maybe the hot air balloon was not his fault. Maybe the equipment was faulty. This idea pleased him.

Perhaps he should have sent Vivian to Universal Studios after all. He didn't think Julia would last. Sometimes Julia got the idea into her head that she was going to help people, save people, and then she would bow out when her plan was not working out the way she'd thought it would. Jonathan did not think that three days at Universal Studios were going to agree with her. He had told her this and she had said that the average trip lasted a week. He was always frustrated when he knew that he was right and Julia didn't listen to him. She almost never admitted being in the wrong.

The mother was going to be exhausted.

It had seemed like a sign, finding her awake at three in the morning, but maybe he had been too quick to give in to his desires.

It was not that Joannie needed actual saving. Alone in the house, he had googled her, and apparently she was a somewhat successful novelist. She had won awards, even. This surprised Jonathan because she did not come across as a successful person. She had an air of quiet desperation that Jonathan found appealing. Maybe he was like Julia in that way. They both loved the idea of saving people, but it was harder to do than it appeared. All too often, people turned out to be ungrateful, unwilling to change.

He had a good feeling about Joannie, though.

She was worth the risk. Like Vivian was worth the risk.

He had brought these women into his home.

Jonathan had never made silent love before and it had been exhilarating. It was as if all sexual experiences should have some kind of obstruction, to enliven them, make them that much better. In this case, complete silence. He could see how turned on she was, and still, she did not gasp, she did not moan, but all the feeling was there in her eyes, in the tension in her body. Electric. That made him more excited. Even though he did not find her particularly attractive, it was thrilling how much she wanted him.

Joannie, he supposed, was actually desperate. Which was sort of not cool. He would talk to his therapist about that during their next session. He never knew what to talk about, only that Julia had told him to see a therapist. He knew that his therapist both liked and loathed him, and he kept her interested with the stories he told. He was no Tony Soprano—he did not have people whacked—but he was not an altar boy either. There was so much he could not tell his therapist. Not his sometimes unethical business practices. Not his feelings for Vivian. There was so much he did not tell her that it really was a waste of money.

He looked at images of Joannie on the screen. She was younger when she published the book. Thinner. Hotter. He found a picture of her with her ex-husband. Dude had a beard. Long hair. Clearly not good enough for her.

"Oh, Joannie," he said.

Joannie's little girl was adorable. That was part of his attraction to Joannie. The mother/daughter package. That had been the plan with Julia. To have an adorable, articulate, intelligent perfect child of their own. He had believed, rich as they were, that somehow they could make that work, but no amount of money could make Julia's eggs viable. So Julia landed on the terrible idea that she wanted a Vietnamese baby, and he wanted a surrogate. They were at an impasse. So it had seemed, for a beautiful minute, that it might be a good idea to sort of adopt them both: the girl and her mother. But it was after fucking the mother, after having had some time to himself, that he realized that this was a plan that would not work. Because the mother, Joannie, was a person. She was sensitive. As women tended to be. She was going to want love. Real love. The kind he had only for Julia.

He was afraid that Vivian had also become confused, mistaking his affection for something more. They both loved Vivian, Jonathan and Julia, but he had seen her looking at him. She had criticized him, too, for the affairs, something that was not her place. "Really, Jonathan?" she had said, texting him the link to the Page Six story. He probably should have fired her then. For all he knew, she had placed it.

He didn't fire her. She was a kid. She felt strongly about things. Besides, it was just a suspicion. She had told him her bizarro plans to go to graduate school, to get an MFA. "Noooo," he had told her. "So many fucking people want to be writers," he said. "Too many writers per capita for how many people actually read books."

"Thank you for crushing my dreams," she said.

That was not the first time he had noticed her anger.

Vivian. She was not close to her parents, another reason he and Julia should not adopt. Another reason he should give Vivian advice, as much as she might not want to hear it. Who else was going to guide her?

It was not like Jonathan to be reflective. Had the hot air balloon crash *changed* him? That was absurd. He needed to do something. Play tennis. Go into the city. To the office. Call Selina, even though it was Selina who had gotten him into trouble. She was done with him after that story in the paper. Fair enough. Jonathan needed to not do anything, Julia told him, patting his knee, something that was hard for him.

Suddenly, Jonathan had a brilliant idea, something he could do, something perfect to fix things with the assistant who had grown so displeased with him. Jonathan could give her Joannie. Vivian had actually read her novel. She had loved it. What were the odds? He could pay Joannie to coach Vivian, read her writing, give her praise. No one wanted to be a charity case. He had a job for Joannie. An actual job. He could give Vivian a writing teacher. This was better than any graduate school. Private! Exclusive! Award-winning!

Then she would not want to leave.

Jonathan could feel her wanting to leave.

He didn't understand.

He didn't understand why he was so desperate for her to stay. His feelings, he told Joannie, were not inappropriate. He was not that guy. Vivian was their Vietnamese orphan. She was theirs. They both loved and adored her. Jonathan wondered why it had taken him so long to realize that. Why did Julia not see it? Vivian was *theirs*.

Vivian had bought Jonathan a bagel with lox and a bagel-store coffee. This, she knew, was one of his favorite meals.

But he had also gone off carbs, and she knew this, too. He decided that this was not a mistake but, instead, a present. He deserved this bagel. She had no idea what the last two days had been like. The humiliation of the hot air balloon, of that Johnny asshole having sex with his wife. No, he was not over that. He had evened the score last night but somehow did not feel any better. The bagel was good. So good. Vivian understood him.

He could also imagine what Vivian would say if he were to show her his gratitude for this bagel, tell her his feelings. *It's just a bagel,* she would say. They ate in silence. He realized he was having an entire conversation with Vivian in his head. It was another beautiful day. Vivian had bought herself a fruit salad. She also was not eating carbs. Maybe the bagel was not a reward. Maybe, in fact, it was a spiteful gesture. He wanted a fruit salad, too.

"Did you get any fruit for me?"

Vivian shook her head.

So many responses crowded Jonathan's brain. Was he really going to get into an argument with her over fruit salad?

"They're coming back tomorrow morning," Vivian said.

"What?" Jonathan was surprised. "Already?"

He knew it; he knew that Julia would not last. He wondered how bad it had been. He should have gone. For Julia's sake. "Do you know what happened?" he asked. "What did Julia tell you?"

He was hurt, of course, that Vivian knew and he didn't. Vivian was mad at him, and she had to get over it. It might feel like she was family, but she was an employee. He had to remind himself of this fact, over and over again. He heard Julia's voice in his head. It strangely felt like the sky was falling.

"Lucy fell," Vivian said. "Apparently, she got upset about something and started to run and she fell down."

"Did she hurt herself?"

"Scrapes," Vivian said, nodding. "Bruises. Nothing serious. I think she scared herself. She wanted to leave. And Julia wanted to come back anyway."

Jonathan let out a deep breath. Everyone was fine. Vivian did not hate him. Julia was coming back. He should never have let them go. He could have taken Lucy out on his boat.

"Of course she did," Jonathan said. Vivian was picking at her fruit, unconcerned, almost bored with the conversation. Her lack of enthusiasm bordered on insolence. "They are all okay?" he repeated.

"Why wouldn't they be?"

The change in Vivian was jarring. Jonathan did not know what to make of all this attitude. Sure, she was basically a kid. A moody teenager. But why was she so angry? At Jonathan of all people? He could ask her, of course, but was he ready for her answer? Usually their daily meeting was something he looked forward to. Some days he was all business, but out at the pool, it was supposed to feel leisurely. Pleasant. It was a beautiful day, Jonathan reminded himself. He was confused. She had barely touched her fruit salad, and the bagel store made a good one. Mangos. Raspberries. Jonathan reached for a piece of mango and she actually slapped his hand.

"What?" Jonathan said. "What did you just do?"

"You can't just eat my food without asking," Vivian said.

Jonathan did not know what was happening.

"Vivian," he said.

"Jonathan," she said.

"Do you want to leave?" Jonathan asked. "Do you have somewhere else to be?"

He realized he meant the big picture with this question. But there was only one acceptable answer to his question. No, she did not want to leave. But Vivian stood up. As if to leave. Jonathan's heart started to race. How had he allowed himself to become so vulnerable to this twit of a girl?

"Do you think I am going to quit?" Vivian asked.

Jonathan's leg started to bounce, a nervous tic he had gotten under control. That was exactly what he had thought. That was currently his greatest fear.

"No," he said. "Of course not. Why would you quit?"

Vivian stared at him. She had begun wearing glasses with clunky black frames. Jonathan did not like them. It was harder to read the expression on her face when she wore these glasses. He knew that she was angry, but as he reminded himself, she had no reason to be angry. It was a piece of mango. Why the fuck didn't she buy him a fruit salad?

"It's not a big thing," Vivian said. "I just don't want to be here, when they get back. I don't want to intrude."

Jonathan let out a deep sigh of relief. It came out surprisingly loud. The loudness of this exhalation made him remember being with Joannie. The sex. They had been so fucking quiet. They had not woken the girl. Vivian didn't know about this, did she? Vivian had been strange around Joannie at the pool, condescending, out of line. But that was before. She couldn't know. She was in the guesthouse. She would disapprove. She had been complicit in his previous dalliances, making dinner reservations and booking hotel rooms, but it was beginning to seem as if she disapproved. She cared for Julia. Of course she disapproved. Maybe that was where the anger was coming from. Of course, that was it! He had disappointed her. How had he not seen that before? But as his assistant, a paid assistant, she did not have the right to have opinions about his life. She was paid to make dinner reservations.

"You are never an intrusion," Jonathan said, making himself focus on the situation at hand. She had sat back down, but she was purposefully looking away. Jonathan focused his gaze on a raspberry. Vivian had eaten the mango. He loved fruit salad. He would not take the raspberry. It was ridiculous, how much he wanted to, but he wouldn't. He didn't. "You are part of the family, you know."

He had just reminded himself that she was paid to make reservations for him. Therefore not family.

"Jonathan," Vivian said. "Julia and I have both talked to you about this. Boundaries. I work for you. It's nice of you to say and all, but I am not family. I already have a family."

"You have talked to me, I know. I'm genuinely making an effort. I don't see the need for you to constantly point this out. This is not a typical office job. You live here. This is your home. Our boundaries are going to be fluid. I care about you. We are a family."

Vivian shook her head. She turned red, in fact, as if she was going to explode. Okay, fine, Vivian required boundaries. It's not as if she didn't have days off. She no longer responded to texts after certain hours. She would continue to do extremely personal things for him; that was actually part of her job. It was not her place to disapprove. Or make those snarky little faces.

"You have to try harder," Vivian said. "I'm not your wife."

"God," Jonathan said. "I know that. I already have a wife."

"I care about Julia," Vivian said. "I don't like how you are treating her."

Jonathan scratched his head. "That is not your place to say."

"Can I go now?" Vivian asked.

"No," he said.

"No?" Vivian said.

"No," Jonathan said, even though he also wanted her to go. But he couldn't leave it like this. He felt like he was back in the hot air balloon, veering dangerously off course.

Jonathan remembered his idea.

"No," Jonathan said. "We have more to talk about."

"Fine," Vivian said.

"Fine," Jonathan said.

He looked at her. She was waiting. She had not eaten the last raspberry. It was going to torment him.

"So, you read Joannie's book," he said, trying to keep the tone of his voice light, casual. "Was it good?"

Vivian nodded. She seemed surprised that this was what he wanted to talk about and hesitated before answering. "It's good."

"Perfect!" Jonathan actually punched the table. "It's good. I was worried you were going to say it was a piece of shit. I think we should all read it together."

Vivian pushed a strand of hair behind her ear. More than eating that raspberry, he wanted to touch her hair. This would be considered off-limits.

"I think technically the book is still good," Vivian said carefully. "I read it a long time ago and it would be different if I read it now. Once you meet the author, everything changes. I know too much about her."

Jonathan went blank. What she'd said made no sense to him, but at least they were talking in a way that felt almost normal. "I had this idea," Jonathan said. "She could give you writing lessons. She teaches, you know. I bet she is a very good teacher. You don't need an MFA to be a writer."

"Oh my God, Jonathan, I don't need you to find me a writing teacher. Weren't you listening to me?"

"I was!"

"This is not like learning the piano. I told you already, I'm applying to graduate school. I'm working on my writing sample and then applying in the fall."

"Well, that's great," Jonathan said. "I admire your ambition. But you don't know if you'll get in. I mean, who says you can write? It's stupid to go into debt to be a writer. Life is expensive."

Vivian stared at him. "Thanks, Dad," she said.

"I bet Joannie could help you. With your sample, even. She's a real writer. A published writer."

Vivian shook her head. "I don't need you to set me up with one of your women. Jesus, Jonathan."

"What?" Jonathan said. "What are you talking about?"

Vivian stared at him, looked away. She ate the last raspberry, and maybe she knew how much he wanted it. She seemed stronger, more confident. She was able to make eye contact again.

"I can almost understand about the models," she said. "And that actress. Like candy. But—"

Vivian stopped there.

"Go on," Jonathan said. "But . . ."

"But her? A single mother, Jonathan," Vivian said. "That's different. That's not okay."

"Are you passing judgment about my behavior?"

Vivian's chin had started to quiver.

"Are you?"

"It's disgusting, really," Vivian said. "You know it is."

"I know no such thing."

Jonathan gave Vivian a chance to take it back. She didn't. How could she even know?

"How do you know?" he said. "How do you know?"

Vivian did not answer.

"Answer the question."

"There are cameras," she said. "In every room of this house."

Jonathan was stunned. He did not know what to say. He had always thought that she might like him. In an inappropriate way. That she had looked at him that way. Cared too much about what he did and said. That there was a bigger reason for boundaries. But this was too much. A violation. Jonathan did not have words. He took the remaining half of his bagel and he threw it. They both watched it land in the pool and sink to the bottom. He thought of the hot air balloon. The way he could have sunk, if Joannie had not saved him.

The bagel just lay there. He could have thrown it onto the grass. It could have been food for the birds. Now it was a mess to be cleaned up.

"I am not eating gluten," he said. This was what came out of his mouth. "I have told you that. This is a job. Do your fucking job."

"Okay," Vivian said. She did not, however, apologize. Nor did she move. He was not going to retrieve the bagel, that was for sure. "Anything else?" she asked.

"Order three copies of Joannie's book."

"What?"

"One of them is for you."

"For me," she said. "Seriously? I told you. I've already read it. She's a has-been. A cautionary tale. I wish I had never met her."

"We could have Joannie read from the book," Jonathan said, ignoring her. He was somehow still stuck on the idea of Joannie teaching Vivian. He was, he supposed, trying to save the situation. "She could give a reading at the pool. It would be—what's the word?—literary. We'll light candles."

Vivian looked at him with disgust. She loathed him. This broke his heart. He wanted her to adore him. She used to worship him.

"I don't want to work for you anymore," she said.

"Too bad," Jonathan responded, not missing a beat. "I'm not firing you."

"I quit," Vivian said.

"Nope," Jonathan said. "I don't accept your resignation."

"I told the newspaper about you," she said. "About Selina. That was me."

Jonathan sighed. He had been right. The damage was done. The damage was minimal. She did not get to quit. He would fire her when he wanted to fire her. At this moment in time, he was not going to give her the satisfaction. "I get it."

"What do you get?"

Jonathan felt sorry for her. It looked like, any second, she was going to break down.

"You're young, Vivvy," he said. He knew that he was not supposed to call her that. "You're idealistic. I have disappointed you. I'm sorry. I want to go back. Forget about all of this. I forgive you. I blame it all on the hot air balloon."

"No," Vivian said. "I betrayed you. I spied on you. You have to fire me."

Jonathan knew that she was right. He had no choice but to fire her. The things she had done were reprehensible. Criminal. He remembered then, about the money, the money she had been stealing. Taking it from his desk, returning it. The torment she must have been going through. He had enjoyed it. It was not as if she was the only one checking the security cameras. He imagined Julia coming home, exhausted, and having to tell her that Vivian was leaving. She would kill him.

"I am not firing you," Jonathan said.

"Then I quit!" Vivian said, her voice firm. She was trying, he realized, to hold her own. Against him.

"Oh, Vivian." Jonathan looked at her. He reached over and took off her glasses. He did not give a shit anymore about boundaries. He wanted to see her face. Her beautiful face. Her almond eyes. The long lashes. Fuck it. He stroked her long, shiny hair. It was as soft as he'd thought it would be. "Like I said, I don't accept your resignation."

"I don't care," Vivian said. Tears started to stream down her cheeks. She was really hurting. Jonathan did not want to hurt her. But she couldn't leave. The idea was unimaginable to Jonathan. Losing her. He was not going to lose her. He was not going to lose Julia either. Sometimes in life you had to put up with things. He wiped the tears from her face as they fell.

"I love you, Viv," he said.

"I don't care," she said.

"You love me, too," he said.

"It doesn't matter," she said.

"I know you have been stealing," he said. "I have all the footage."

Vivian's eyes opened wide.

"What?" she said.

"I watch the cameras, too," he said. "Ten thousand dollars."

"I put it back," she said. "All of it. Or I will. I always put it back."

"Maybe." Jonathan shrugged. "The desk is empty. I can show the tape to the police," Jonathan said. "And to Julia. What will she think, after everything we have done for you?"

"Don't," Vivian whispered.

"Maybe I'll call your parents," he said. "They might be interested to hear about your job performance."

It felt good, putting Vivian back in her place. Exerting his power over her once again. It had not needed to go this far. She had brought them to this moment. Jonathan put Vivian's glasses back on her face. Boundaries. He could hear Julia's voice. He had ideas about what she would think about what had just happened, there at the pool on a beautiful day, but he wasn't going to be telling her. He did not think Vivian would either. From now on, he was going to respect her boundaries.

"I am going to forget about everything we've said just now," Jonathan said. "Clean slate. I suggest you do the same."

Vivian didn't say anything.

"Vivian?" he asked.

"We're going to forget," she said.

"And you're not going to quit," he said.

"No," Vivian said.

"If you don't mind," Jonathan said, "I'd like for you to do your job. Get the bagel out of the pool. The skimmer is in the shed. Behind the gatehouse. You know where it is."

Vivian nodded.

"You can keep the money," he said. "You've earned it."

Vivian's jaw dropped.

"And forget about the books," Jonathan said. "Don't order them. I changed my mind about that. I don't think you want writing lessons."

"I don't," Vivian said.

"Okay." Jonathan clapped his hands. "Good. That's settled. It's better when it's just the three of us. Don't you think?"

Jonathan wondered what his therapist would think about this. This conversation. He wasn't going to tell her. Sometimes, when necessary, he could be a son of a bitch. He felt bad for the writer, the mother. Joannie. She had told him she loved him. She was cute, really. Adorable. Surprisingly good in bed. But too much trouble.

"I've gotta go. I have tennis in half an hour. Clean up the bagel," he said. "And, Vivian," he added.

"Yes?" Her voice was small; she was looking down.

It wouldn't be the same after this, but he wasn't ready to let her go. He would, eventually, and he would give her a bonus. A glowing recommendation if she ever asked for one. She could go to graduate school if she really wanted to, and now she would have something to write about. She would be fine. He was sure about it.

"No more carbs," he said.

Julia

Julia found that other people were a source of constant irritation. She had done this thing: taken Lucy to the place where she most wanted to go in all the world, and the little girl had loved it, too. Her mother just couldn't cut it. Julia couldn't cut it either, but she wasn't the girl's mother. Why couldn't Joannie suck it up?

"We have to know our limitations," Julia said.

There was no point in telling this woman off, telling her that she was a disappointment. In the course of her life, Julia had learned that most people could not take the truth.

Joannie agreed. "I'm painfully aware."

It was easy enough to change the flights. She had Vivian do

it. Vivian was the one person who did not let her down. Julia wondered if it was Jonathan who had sabotaged this trip. If he had come, gone on one fucking ride with Lucy, maybe they could have lasted another day. Julia had wanted to give the girl a magical experience, and she couldn't do it. Because the place was a horror. They were so lucky Lucy didn't get hurt on that crazed run of hers. They were all quiet on the way back to the hotel.

Joannie said they would go to the pool, but Julia decided not to join them. They spoke again before dinner, and Joannie admitted that they wanted to go home. They were ungrateful. Stupid. Annoying. Julia was relieved. She asked Joannie if she wanted to have a drink before they headed out to the restaurant. Julia wanted a drink. She offered Joannie a Ritalin. Or a Xanax. Her choice. "What do you want?" Julia asked. "To go up or down?"

Joannie picked the anxiety pill.

It was, Julia wanted to explain to her, the wrong choice. But Julia had given her the choice. Joannie, of course, should have taken the speed. It gave Julia focus, clarity. She had felt generous in her willingness to share. It was prescription medication, after all.

They ate at the restaurant that Lucy had picked, the Rainforest Café. "Nora went here! Nora went here!" Lucy screamed on the drive to the restaurant. Julia had thought Lucy was different than other children, a child who did not scream. Maybe there was no such thing.

It was an atrocious restaurant, designed to be a veritable indoor jungle. But Joannie had taken her pill, Julia had taken hers, and throughout the course of the meal, they had three cold beers apiece. It was the kind of restaurant that would have made them both otherwise lose their minds: it had an artificial waterfall, animatronic animals, perky waitresses, plastic plants, laminated menus. Actual piped-in noise, a bird soundtrack with the occasional monkey, the sound of the rain. There were children screaming, babies crying. A contemporary version of hell, comparable to Hogwarts. But they were both at just the right level of inebriation, something Julia was especially skilled at. "We stop at three," Julia said, holding out her hand, as if to physically demonstrate the limit. She felt better, knowing she was going home the next day.

"I am at the perfect level of drunk," Joannie said.

Julia realized that she preferred Joannie drunk. Her husband had wanted to fuck this woman, which meant that Julia should actually pay attention to her in a way that she had yet to do.

"Are you drunk, Mommy?" Lucy asked.

"Of course not, baby," Joannie said.

Julia was also surprised by how quickly Joannie lied, and how stupid it was, to lie to her child, since she had just said that she was drunk. She wondered what else Joannie lied about. She had not forgotten that kiss at the swimming pool, Joannie's leg against Jonathan's in the limo. It occurred to Julia, finishing her third beer, that Joannie's sad, sweet act was utter bullshit.

"Do you like it here?" Joannie asked Lucy, spreading her arms, indicating the atrocious restaurant.

"I love it here," Lucy said. "I love it."

Joannie took her picture. Julia took Joannie's phone and took their picture together. Then a picture of Lucy. They even took a picture of the three of them. The trip was not a total loss. It was important to make sacrifices for other people. "She loves it here!" Joannie said to Julia, obviously pleased. As if Joannie had been redeemed.

"I loved the Hagrid ride, too," Lucy said. "I loved it!"

Lucy would possibly remember all of the right things and none of the wrong ones. The Hagrid. The wands and the cape and the scarf. The butterbeer. The vomit jelly beans. This awful restaurant. The trip was not a total failure.

"Thank you," Joannie mouthed.

Then she said it out loud.

Joannie, at least, was grateful. She even looked happy, the way she wanted to be in the theme park but somehow was unable to fake. "What do you think of Jonathan?" Joannie asked, almost yelling to be heard over the sound of the parrots.

"You mean my husband?" Julia asked. "What do I think of him? Is that what you are asking me?"

Joannie looked away.

Did Joannie really think Julia had forgotten the kiss in the swimming pool? The day *after* the suggested partner swap. Julia didn't think that Joannie, a single mother, a writer, a so-called smart woman, would fall for Jonathan's bullshit. But it appeared she had. Of course she had.

Julia had, at least, warned Vivian, and Vivian had listened. Julia had set the boundaries. Jonathan could not touch her shining black hair, tempting as it was. Call her pet names. Vivian could not fall for his charms.

"I like my husband just fine," Julia said now to Joannie, and that was the end of the conversation.

"Do we fly back first-class?" Lucy asked.

Julia nodded. "We do," she said.

The girl was officially ruined, would always remember what it was like to fly first-class. Some rich people didn't even shell out for first class because it cost so much. Julia was tempted to change the ticket again, put Joannie and Lucy in the cheap seats. One text to Vivian. It could be worth it to see the shock on their faces. What did she think about Jonathan? Julia was surprised by how disappointed she felt in Joannie. She did not have friendships with women, and now she remembered why.

Joannie offered to pay for dinner.

"Why would you do that?" Julia asked.

It was another example of stupidity. Pride. Joannie was a single mother, and Julia was a billionaire. But she let Joannie pay. She saw Joannie make a face when she was given the check, but she handed over her credit card without a word. Idiot. Bad mother.

Julia couldn't sleep.

She was trilling with anger.

She felt used, exploited, misunderstood.

Joannie thought everything was about her. Her loneliness. Her poverty. Her neurotic daughter. She did not think, *Is Julia enjoying this trip? What can I do for Julia?*

Honestly, did she think Julia wanted to do any of the things they did on that trip? An amusement park. The gift shop.

Rainforest restaurant. She was doing it all for *her* kid. Julia didn't have a kid. She was pretty convinced that she had been right all along in not wanting one. That was what she had told herself for her first thirty-eight years of life, and then she had gotten confused.

Julia had to know herself. Accept her limitations. No kid. No Vietnamese orphan. Instead, she would rescue some more cats. That's why she had convinced Jonathan to get out of the city, gotten all that land. She wanted more cats. She did not tell him that, not in so many words. But Jonathan also loved the cats. That was the thing. They were suited to each other. Got along. Better than other people.

It was stupid to be angry at Joannie because of Jonathan. Julia had offered up her husband as a gift, and Joannie had believed that the offer was real. She was as awful as anybody else. Julia would show her. She knocked on Joannie's door. It was one in the morning, but Joannie was awake. Lucy was asleep, sprawled out on the bed. Joannie's eyes widened, but she invited her in.

"You share a bed with that?" Julia asked.

"I should have specified double beds."

"Seriously," Julia said. "Why don't you ask for what you need?"

Joannie shrugged. "Who are you, really, to be giving me anything?" she said.

It was true. Only Julia hadn't realized that Joannie had also realized it. Julia had crossed a line, inserting herself into Joannie's life, making decisions, spending money. Jonathan, too. His smarmy line directed at Lucy. *I have a boat with a waterslide.* Clearly, they had no lasting interest in these people.

"Do you want something to drink?" Joannie asked her.

Julia went over to the mini fridge. She found mini bottles of Jameson. Dark chocolate salted caramels. She gave Joannie a mini bottle and opened the chocolates, and they settled on the couch.

"TV?" Julia asked.

Joannie nodded to her daughter. "Don't want to wake her up. We have to be quiet."

No TV. Fine. That wasn't why she was there.

"Did you sleep with my husband?" Julia asked.

Joannie coughed up her whiskey.

"I guess that's my answer?"

Tears welled in Joannie eyes. Maybe because she was choking, couldn't breathe. Julia wondered if she would have to perform the Heimlich maneuver on her. She did not want the girl to grow up without a mother. Joannie held up her hand.

She got up off the couch and took a lap around the room, catching her breath.

Julia waited. She wondered when they had done it. At the house, before the lobster? After the lobster? She had fed them lobster. The guest room was at the back of the house, separate from Julia and Jonathan. He could have gone there, but is that where they fucked? This woman would not even turn on the TV for fear of waking her daughter.

"Are you okay?" she asked Joannie.

Joannie nodded. Her face was bright red. It looked like she was breathing almost normally again.

"So you did sleep with him? That's a yes?"

Joannie nodded. She would have been smarter to lie, but then the choking had given her away.

"You probably thought it was okay," Julia said. "Because I suggested the swap, the night before."

Joannie nodded again. She looked afraid. Often, people were afraid of Julia. They were wrong, of course. Julia was literally the nicest person on the planet, and she would do anything for you, anything—if you did not betray her.

They were sitting next to each other on the couch again. Julia could smell Joannie's fear. "You know what's funny?" Julia asked.

Joannie did not say anything at all.

"What's funny is that I thought you were attracted to me."

Joannie nodded. She had lost her ability to speak.

"You *were* attracted to me?"

Joannie nodded again.

"So that's a yes."

Julia had been right about this. She had had a girlfriend in college. They had been roommates for two years and then lived together their first year after college. Julia had been in love, but the girlfriend left her for another woman. This had entirely crushed Julia's idea of lesbians. She thought women were supposed *to be better*. She took Joannie's face in her hands and she kissed her. Joannie did not respond. She did not reject or return the kiss. In fact, she had started to shake.

"I am not going to bite," Julia said, still holding her face in her hands.

"I know," Joannie said.

She was right, though, to be worried. Julia could bite.

"Let's try it again?" Julia said.

Joannie nodded.

Clearly, she was not an articulate person. Probably, Julia thought, that was why she was a writer.

"We'll try it again," Julia whispered, because Joannie needed a little more coaxing.

Joannie nodded. She was sweet in her nervousness, like a little girl.

"Okay," Julia said. "On the count of three."

Joannie laughed.

"That's better."

Julia counted to three. She leaned in again and kissed the woman who had fucked her husband. She put her tongue in Joannie's mouth. She caressed the back of her head. She could feel Joannie unclench, relax. Return the kiss. She kept kissing. It was a little bit like kissing herself. A soft moan escaped from Joannie's lips.

Julia kissed Joannie's throat, her collarbone.

This felt good. Julia was proving something to herself.

She was better than Jonathan. She could, she knew, take this experiment further. She could caress Joannie's breasts, put her hand down Joannie's pajama pants, slide a finger into her vagina. She was sure somehow that Joannie was wet. But she wasn't going to do that. Because she wasn't an asshole. Not like her husband. She pulled away.

"Good night, Joannie."

Julia stood up. She caught her breath. Maybe she had been a little bit turned on, too, but no. Not by her. Not by this sad pathetic woman. She was not going to keep them, the girl and her mother, like pets. She already had pets.

Joannie looked at her. The poor woman still couldn't talk.

Julia had rendered her mute.

"I'll see you in the morning," Julia said. "I'll let you know when the car is coming."

Julia felt better. She was sure she would be able to sleep. She was happy to be going home. She loved her cats. Her cats never disappointed her. She nursed sick cats back to health. She would get more of them, more cats. She missed her cats. She would be the craziest cat lady on the planet. What the fuck did she care? She was going home soon. To her cats. Who must be missing her.

She knew her limitations.

Joannie

J oannie had fucked Julia's husband, and now she felt like she had just been fucked by Julia. She did not even know what had happened. She said nothing as Julia walked away, closed the door behind her.

"What?" Lucy said, waking up. "What happened?"

"Nothing," Joannie said, hurrying into the bed. "Make room for me. You are asleep."

"I'm not," Lucy said.

"You were asleep," she said. "You'll fall right back asleep."

Joannie spooned Lucy and much to her relief, Lucy did fall right back asleep. She had slept through the defining events of the weekend, and Joannie was grateful. They were going to make it through, basically unscathed. She hoped. There was still the flight home. The possibility of literally crashing and burning, their remains scattered in the Atlantic Ocean.

She could not fall asleep.

She could not risk getting back out of bed. She was a piece of shit. That's how she felt. The phrase that kept running through her head. A piece of shit. The worst mother ever. She settled on that. Three in the morning was her worst time of the day, the time that she was cruelest to herself. She could not believe anything she told herself. This, Joannie knew, was the time when she told herself that she would never write again, that she would never be able to support her daughter, that she would never move out of her crappy apartment, that she had no right to live.

It had been three in the morning when she had sex with Jonathan Foster. Clearly, another bad decision. Joannie knew, or at least she hoped, that when she woke up in the morning, she would not feel this bad.

She should never listen to the voice in her head.

That had been so humiliating with Julia.

A humiliation she had not known before.

Fuck.

Her entire future, and Lucy's future, depended on her writing another novel and then selling it, and it turned out that that was too much pressure. She had not risen to the occasion. In the past, Joannie had thrived on pressure. That was how she had finished her first book, the one that had won a fucking prize, sold thousands of copies, supposedly securing her future, except that she had gone on from there to fuck it up.

Lost confidence in herself and produced nothing. Not a goddamned thing. She could blame it on the pandemic, but what
good did that do her?

A long time ago, right after her divorce, her mother's childhood best friend had invited Joannie and Lucy to spend a
weekend at her house in the Hamptons. This woman had
spoiled Joannie in the best possible way, cooked them wonderful meals, drove them to beaches, let them swim in her
pool, made them popcorn for a movie night in her living room,
served homemade granola for breakfast—and then told Joannie as she drove her back to the train, in no uncertain terms,
that Joannie needed to get a job. A real, full-time job, with
benefits and an actual salary. "A job?" Joannie actually gasped,
as if it was tantamount to torture. The idea of it. The idea of
going back to work. Working for someone else. Putting Lucy
in daycare, not taking care of her daughter. What could she
even do?

She had done it before. Retail jobs. Office jobs. She was
even good at it until she wasn't. "Self-sabotage," her last real
boss had told her before firing her. "You do the work incredibly well, until you don't do any work at all."

It felt like she had been stabbed in the gut. This rich
woman, a true housewife, supported by her successful doctor husband, telling her to get a job. It had been the greatest
motivator. Joannie had finished her book and sold it, and like
a miracle, it had done well, and she had lived off that money
for a very long time, and now it had run out. She was teaching
and editing and she was nowhere near finishing another book.
She was going to have to snap out of it.

She had never been invited back to the Hamptons. She had reached out, but the next invitation had not been forthcoming. Joannie never knew why.

That meal at the rainforest restaurant had cost her close to two hundred dollars. All those beers. She shouldn't have paid for it. She'd put it on her credit card, which she was already unable to pay off. Pride was a stupid thing. It would get her nowhere.

She had been wrong about so many things.

She had told Jonathan Foster that she *loved* him.

The worst thing was that in that actual moment, she had meant it. She so desperately wanted someone to take care of her. That wasn't going to happen, and that was okay. It was okay. She was doing it, taking care of herself. Her daughter. It would be better if she never saw him again. Or Julia. She would have to see her. In the morning. It was the middle of the night, and Joannie was sure that she would not sleep. But even with no sleep, it would still be a new day.

Joannie had not slept well, possibly, in years. She tried counting backward from eight hundred; she took deep breaths. She was going to have to get a job after all. It was okay. Most people had jobs. She might like a job. She would have a reason to brush her hair, change her clothes. Get new clothes. She used to like, back when she had jobs, going out to lunch.

The alarm clock went off, waking her up.

It was so easy to pack, they had packed so little, and there were still two hours before they had to leave for the airport.

Joannie had set the alarm early, not knowing that she would have such a terrible night. She had wanted to give herself some time to swim in the hotel pool, which would not be crowded so early in the morning.

Only Lucy refused to go.

"My Band-Aids will come off," she insisted.

Joannie had her suit on. Her goggles. She had already applied sunblock. "I won't go!" Lucy screamed.

The idea of being forced to swim in a hotel pool made Lucy cry. Joannie could not believe it. Drastic action was called for. Joannie texted Julia, asking if she could leave Lucy with her for an hour, and Julia texted back no.

No.

She texted back *no.*

Joannie so rarely asked for things. She felt like she deserved this one little thing.

No.

Well, she wasn't going to beg. It made Joannie feel glad that she had fucked Julia's husband.

No. She couldn't believe it.

She asked Lucy if Lucy would come down to the pool and sit on a lounge chair while she swam. "You can play on my phone the whole time," she said.

Lucy said no.

"I want to stay in the hotel room."

Joannie knew that she was the mother. She knew that what she said should go, but somehow she couldn't fight with her daughter, force her to go down to the swimming pool. She felt, however, like she was losing her mind.

"Are you sure?" she asked Lucy. "You wouldn't go, just for me? We came all the way to Florida."

"We didn't like the pool," Lucy said. "It was crowded. You didn't like it either."

"But it won't be now. It's morning."

Lucy shook her head. "My Band-Aids," she said.

"I have more Band-Aids," Joannie said. "You are being unreasonable."

"I'm not," Lucy said. "I'm not."

Joannie remembered again how two nights ago she had had sex in the same room as her daughter in the middle of the night. That was not reasonable. Last night, at least, she had done nothing inappropriate. She thought about leaving Lucy alone in the room while she went down to swim, but she wouldn't do that. She wasn't even considering it. It was just an idea. A bad idea.

Joannie took a deep breath.

Her head hurt.

"I am going to take a bath," Joannie said. She wondered why this had not occurred to her in the first place. It was a Jacuzzi tub. The night before, she had been too tired when they got back from dinner to take a bath. That had been stupid. It was a beautiful bathtub.

"I don't want you to," Lucy said.

"You don't?"

Lucy shook her head. Another no.

"Why not?"

"Because I will be jealous."

"Then join me, Lucy. In the bath."

They often took baths together.

"My Band-Aids," Lucy said.

"Lucy," Joannie said. "That's not fair."

"I know," Lucy said.

"Then can you be fair?" Joannie said. "I already gave up the swimming pool."

"I scraped myself," Lucy said. "My knees and my hands. I hurt myself. It still stings. The water will sting. I can't go in."

"The water will feel good."

Lucy shook her head. "It's going to sting."

Maybe Lucy was right. Maybe the water *was* going to sting.

"My head is pounding," Joannie said. "I just need to put my head under the water."

She walked into the bathroom and turned on the water. Lucy followed her. "Why is your head pounding?"

"I had a bad night's sleep."

"Why did you have a bad night's sleep?" Lucy asked.

"I don't know, baby. I just did."

"Because you got drunk," Lucy said.

Lucy had heard her at the restaurant. Of course she had. It would be stupid to deny it. She was a bad mother. She loved Lucy so much and still she was a bad mother. But that was not why her head hurt. Her head hurt because she needed more sleep.

They both stood by the enormous tub, watching it fill.

"We are going to miss the plane," Lucy said.

"We are not going to miss the plane. I set the alarm early."

"We will," Lucy said. "We have to get to the airport early."

"I know we have to get to the airport early," Joannie said.

"I know when we have to leave. There is time for a bath. You love baths."

"No," Lucy said.

The tub continued to fill.

Joannie pressed the button for the Jacuzzi bubbles.

"Look at that!" she said.

The bubbles came on strong.

"Doesn't that look amazing?" she asked.

"No," Lucy said.

Joannie still couldn't believe that Julia had not agreed to watch Lucy for an hour. Even half an hour. She had said no. No. Julia must really hate her.

"No?" Joannie asked.

"No," Lucy said.

"Go watch TV?" Joannie said.

Lucy shook her head.

"Play on my phone?"

Lucy shook her head.

"Don't you care that my head hurts?" Joannie said. "That this bath will make my head feel better?"

"I do care," Lucy said. "I just don't want you to."

Joannie looked at the water.

"One minute."

Lucy shook her head. "No," she said.

Joannie took off her T-shirt. She took off her pajama bottoms.

"No," Lucy said.

"Just one minute."

"Mom!" Lucy screamed. "I told you no."

Joannie got into the tub and then she lay all the way down and then she sank under the water, letting the bubbles cover her. She already was a terrible mother. She could hear Lucy screaming, "Get out, get out, get out!"

It was less loud, because she was underwater.

Joannie held her breath. She counted to ten and she resurfaced to Lucy's screaming.

"Hey, baby," she said. "It's so nice. Just a little bit longer."

Joannie took the deepest breath and went back under. The water was so hot. The bubbles were so strong. It was a wonderful bathtub and she was glad that she had taken the bath, because she'd had to. She also felt as guilty as she had ever felt. She came back up for air.

"Done!" she said, triumphantly.

Joannie got out of the tub. She wrapped herself in a large white hotel towel. It was a wonderful towel. It was a wonderful hotel room. Joannie had flown first-class for the first time, but maybe that was not a good thing. She was forever ruined, and probably forever angry, too, knowing just how nice it was.

"I love you, Lucy," Joannie said, hugging her daughter.

She could feel Lucy soften in her arms. Lucy did not like to hold a grudge. Lucy simply wanted her mother when she wanted her. Joannie knew that. Joannie felt lucky. So incredibly lucky. She had taken an enormous risk, getting into the bath. Her pounding head had required it. She had needed to go underwater, but she had come back. "Let's watch TV until we have to leave for the airport."

"I want to go home," Lucy said.

"Me, too," Joannie said. She kissed Lucy on the top of her

head. "Let's go home," she said. "Let's get home and get some cats."

"But we can't have cats in our building," Lucy said.

"That's okay," Joannie said.

It was not three in the morning. It was a new day. She thought about her mother's friend, the one who'd told her she needed to get a job, what she could have said. What she had not said. *Don't worry, sweetie. I love you. I'll catch you if you fall.* It was amazing to think how angry Joannie was, so many years later. She had wanted this woman with the house in the Hamptons to be her mother. Her other mother. Her rich mother. Julia, too. In the end, she had never met a rich person she liked. "We'll move," she said. "I promise."

She had made a promise, in the act of giving birth to Lucy. A promise not to fail.

Jonathan

Jonathan knew what time the flight was coming in. He felt annoyed, wondering if he had to be there when they got back. Vivian would tell him to. Sanctimonious twit. They had, at least, reached an understanding. But what had he actually promised Joannie? Her girl? Nothing. A boat trip. An unspecified reward. Honestly, she had not saved his life. He would not have drowned. If she had not jumped into the pool, he would have surfaced, pulled himself out of the water. He had no doubt.

What a fucking weekend.

Julia was going to kill him.

She was going to kill him and then she was going to threaten to leave him, but she would stay. When would she ever find anyone else who understood her the way he did? They could not raise Joannie's daughter. He didn't ever want to see Joannie again, let alone read her book.

On Mondays, he played tennis with his friend Bill. That was what he would do. Jonathan's tennis had improved over the pandemic. Later, he would talk to Julia about some kind of reward for Joannie and she would know what to do. She was a philanthropist. She could invent a mother-artist grant. And if she still wanted a Vietnamese baby, he would agree to it. He had come around on this on his own. He had crossed some boundaries with Vivian, and if confronted, he would own it. Come clean. The girl had been stealing from him for months. He would not press charges against her. So who was the asshole? Sure, he'd left the money in the desk drawer to tempt her, but she had failed miserably.

It was like Julia had told him, he had his limitations.

Johnny

J ohnny got a text from Joannie. But it was actually Lucy, using her mother's phone.

Is Tyson free for a playdate?

R U back? Johnny wrote back.

It had stung, the way they had all left, leaving piles of laundry and a sink full of dirty dishes. He had left the mess behind and gone to Tyson's soccer game. The other team had won 10 to 0. Johnny had felt strangely relieved, that his son was on the losing team. He had looked at the boys on the winning team, so pleased with themselves, and he'd hated them. These boys who were going to be bullies, go to Ivy League schools, the kind who raped girls at frat parties. Fern had really gotten into his head. That was for sure. His son was better than that. His son was like him. Sensitive. Kind. Johnny loved and respected women. Tyson made friends with girls. Like Lucy. Lucy was adorable. He had really blown it with her mother.

Coming home now, Lucy texted.

JOHNNY: Yeah?
LUCY: Yeah
JOHNNY: Come on over. Anytime.
LUCY: Can my mom swim in your pool?
JOHNNY: You bet

Johnny thought about how lovely it was. This little girl, looking out for her mother. For a moment, before the hot air balloon, kissing Joannie, he had imagined their future together, their blended family, forever and ever. Johnny could see himself getting married again. Joannie was a good kisser.

He had made a date at the soccer game. Another mom. Her son's name was Jasper. He was on Tyson's team. He had kicked a goal into his own team's net and all the parents had cheered. It was the only goal they had scored, even if it was for the other team. Jasper's mother was very pretty. She owned a popular ice cream shop in town. She had asked him to come get some ice cream. So maybe it wasn't a date after all.

Julia

fter the flight, Julia realized there was no reason to have brought them back to the house.
But they were almost there before she figured
this out, the car turning down the private road that led to her
house. It didn't matter. She did not have to invite them in. She
had a life to get back to.

Joannie and Lucy could have and should have gone straight
home. They had all their belongings with them. She was surprised Joannie hadn't suggested it, but probably the woman
wanted to see her husband. Good luck with that. Jonathan
wasn't even home. The son of a bitch had texted her that he
had gone to play tennis. Vivian had changed the flights but
had not answered any of Julia's texts since then. That was

unlike Vivian. Leave it to Jonathan to fuck things up with the best assistant they would ever have. She had been gone for one day. She had asked Vivian to make sure lunch was ready, but she would just as soon skip the meal. Eat an early dinner. Joannie and Lucy could find their own lunch. Somewhere else preferably.

She looked at her guests. They looked worn out. Lucy was sunburned, covered in Band-Aids. She was remarkably less cute than she had been the day they met. She had cried during the flight because one of her Band-Aids had come off, disturbing some of the other passengers in first class. Nobody ever cried in first class. The girl's mother, at least, had more Band-Aids in her purse. She was not a terrible mother. Julia spotted one of her favorite cats, Little Kitty, out the car window. Then Samantha, the tabby with three legs. And Mama Cat. Ginger. They were all there. Julia's heart raced. She was home.

Somehow, Joannie didn't realize they were back at the house. The drive back from the airport had been silent. Joannie's eyes had been closed. Lucy was typing on her mother's phone. Neither of them seemed to understand that they had arrived. Julia got out of the car.

"Are we back?" Joannie blinked.

"Driver?" Julia talked to him through his open window. "Do you have time for another stop?"

"Sure thing," he said. "Whatever you need."

It was what Julia hoped he would say.

"Joannie will tell you where she needs to go."

"Not a problem."

Joannie opened her eyes.

"This was fun," Julia told her.

It was, maybe, the most poorly executed lie she had ever told. She felt like she owed them something, but she didn't. She didn't owe them anything. Jonathan had texted about coming up with some kind of reward for saving his life, but Julia didn't think so. She had bought Lucy a ton of shit.

Joannie seemed to be carefully choosing her words.

"Fun," Joannie said.

Joannie had not been able to speak the night before either. Possibly, she wasn't very smart.

"Jonathan," Joannie said, finally understanding what was taking place. "I would like to say thank you before we go. And goodbye."

"He's not home." Julia felt almost giddy.

"He's not?"

"He's playing tennis." The words slid off her tongue.

"Tennis," Joannie repeated.

Julia could not read her expression. What did Joannie think would happen? That they would move into her beautiful home? Swim in her pool, eat her food? More lobster and cheese? These were not real people in need. They were not her family. They were no one to her.

"I want to go home," Lucy said to her mother, tugging on her arm.

Perfect.

It turned out that this was easy. They would go home, back to where they belonged.

Julia walked away before Joannie could respond.

The car drove to the end of the circle and then pulled out of the driveway. It was such a relief to watch them go.

Joannie

Home.

The apartment she hated.

No yard. Nowhere to plant flowers. Not even a flower box out the window. Not enough space inside either. Ugly kitchen cabinets. The duct-taped couch. Lucy was very happy to be back. She had fresh Band-Aids on her knees. She had two new Harry Potter wands and a scarf. She had made a playdate with Tyson. Joannie read the texts Lucy had sent to Johnny on her phone. Lucy had asked if her mother could swim in their pool and he had said yes. Yes. Joannie was all set.

She had a new place to swim until the public pool opened. Maybe it would be awkward, but Joannie did not care. She would swim there anyway. It was a beautiful pool. It was around the corner.

"Can we order sushi for dinner?" Lucy asked.

"Yes!" Joannie said, pleased because it was the perfect idea. "Of course."

She was grateful to be home. Her home. The one that she paid for, even if it was far from perfect. Even if she sometimes hated it. During the pandemic, once it became clear that it was safe to order food, she started ordering sushi all the time, and it had never tasted as good. When she stopped to think about where her money actually went, she knew a lot of it was spent on sushi. Also expensive cups of coffee from the café next door to the Japanese restaurant. Somehow, she would still send Lucy to college. She had time. She would figure it out.

Joannie had not understood, until then, how consumed she had been by self-pity. How needless it had been. How good, even, she had it. And how, aside from Lucy, she would never love again. Joannie had long believed that she was unlovable, and the weekend had confirmed it. That was also fine. She did not think that much of other people either. She wanted only to rely on herself. She was more than competent.

Joannie watered her plants.

She loved her plants.

She wanted to buy more plants.

She loved the armchair she had gotten at a garage sale. She had one good set of sheets with a high thread count, and she made the bed with them. Joannie had not forgotten the promises she had made to herself. A new place to live. A new bed. Cats.

And then she remembered the idea.

The idea in her head.

The idea that had come to her when she was swimming laps. After years of not having any ideas. The idea had not left her. She had not forgotten it. Joannie opened her computer and started to write, even though she only had fifteen minutes before she had to pick up the sushi. She had more ideas. She wrote one sentence and there came the next. Idea after idea. It was like magic. She even had a title. *The Reward*. It was going to be enormous.

Acknowledgments

I want to thank my agent, Alex Glass, who read the first chapter of *Hot Air*, originally a short story, and suggested I turn it into a novel.

My editor, Jenny Jackson, who pushed me to take the story further. She actually wanted a twist, which I thought was impossible, and then, because it was asked of me, I came up with one.

Tiara Sharma, who answered all of my questions, provided edits and invaluable support. I want to thank everyone at Knopf, my publisher, which produces beautiful, beautiful books.

Janet Hansen, who has now designed three outstanding

book covers for my last three novels, including this gorgeous work of art, a deflated rainbow-colored hot air balloon.

Also, Shelley Salamensky, forever my first reader. Emily Sanders Hopkins, who provided the insane writing prompt. Catherine Chung, who provided a room to write in, with a view of an unattainable swimming pool, which worked its way into the plot.

My family—my mother Ann and my sister Julie and my brother Michael—and my daughter Nina, especially, who forced me into the world of cat ownership, which provides a constant source of new material and love and wonder. Thank you, Ginger and Sunshine.

Finally, thanks to so many wonderful booksellers and librarians and readers and reviewers and book influencers and friends who read my books and make me believe that books do matter, bring comfort and joy, and have a place in this ugly, beautiful world we all live in.

A NOTE ABOUT THE AUTHOR

Marcy Dermansky is the author of the critically
acclaimed novels *Hurricane Girl, Very Nice, The Red Car,
Bad Marie,* and *Twins.* She has received fellowships
from MacDowell and the Edward F. Albee Foundation.
She lives with her daughter in Montclair, New Jersey.

A NOTE ON THE TYPE

This book was set in Hoefler Text, a family of fonts
designed by Jonathan Hoefler, who was born in 1970.
First designed in 1991, Hoefler Text was intended
as an advancement on existing desktop computer
typography, including as it does an exponentially
larger number of glyphs than previous fonts. In
form, Hoefler Text looks to the old-style fonts of
the seventeenth century, but it is wholly of its time,
employing a precision and sophistication only
available to the late twentieth century.

Typeset at Scribe
Philadelphia, Pennsylvania

Printed and bound by Berryville Graphics
Berryville, Virginia

Book design by Pei Loi Koay